REVENGE FOR AN ENGLISH LORD

Margaret Nyhon

'[Boarding schools are] Light-houses my boy!
Beacons of the future! Capsules with hundreds of
bright little seeds in each, out of which will spring
the wiser, better England of the future!'

— From Memoirs of Sherlock Holmes

Contents

Introduction

This novel is the sequel to *Betrayal by an Irish Rose*. The family saga continues down through the next generation.

Mary's family were forced to leave Ireland during the potato famine and sail across the Irish Sea to England, where her father could get work in Cornwall in the tin mines. Tragedy followed this family with the death of her mother leaving behind seven children. Mary's decision to leave her life of poverty and go to London to find work led her to a life she could not have dreamt of. She never forgot her hatred for the English gentry, who imported their wheat back to England during the famine instead of leaving it to feed the starving Irish. One day she would return to Ireland; she never forgot her roots.

Her passionate meeting in London with a young Irish lad played a big part in her life, even when she met and married Lord Albert Rothchild. Mary went on to have five children, but to whom did they belong? As the children grew older, the title of Lord was at stake and rightfully belonged to the first-born son, Joseph. But it was the second son, Charles, who lay claim to the peerage, at any cost, this cost being Joseph's life. From that day forth the nightmare continued and after Lord Albert passed away, Charles proclaimed himself Lord Charles Rothchild, giving him much power, which he used and abused.

But in his way stood his mother, Mary, and her Irish lover. Lord Charles hated the Irish, especially the 'Irish curse', the red hair that all other family members had. He was the exception! On turning twenty-one, he was to inherit the Rothchild estate; and now he was free to order his family off his land. But Mary took with her ten of the Irish farms, her entitlement, leaving Lord Charles with eight farms, for which he felt cheated. Thus his hatred for the Irish grew.

The story continues ...

1

Revenge for an English Lord

Charles stood in shock as he learnt from his mother's solicitor that the family were gone, to where he would not divulge. Tears streamed down his face; he didn't think he would feel anything for the Irish, they were gone from his life. This he had secretly hoped for, but now, when the raw facts were before him, he wept. George, his new butler, came to his aid and put his arms around him. Charles took comfort in his arms. Suddenly the tears stopped; this was just a momentary sadness that would pass as quickly as it arrived. The Rothchild estate was now his, there was no trace of any Irish; that had left with his family. He felt they were never really part of the English gentry, it was just because his father, Lord Albert Rothchild, was besotted with an Irish lass that this bloodline had evolved. He was so happy he did not inherit the red Irish hair like his half sister and brothers. To him this was the 'Irish curse' and thankfully it stayed with the Irish and did not cross over to the English side of the family. But then, as he took time and thought back to his elder brother, Joseph, the Irish blood had run through his veins giving him the red hair. Did he feel a moment of guilt as he thought of Joseph? Not a bit. Joseph stood in the way of his 'Lordship' so he had to be dealt to, or rather, he had to be disposed of.

So much had happened in the past, but that was a distant memory; all that he wanted he now owned; well, half of it, as the rest was taken by his mother, Mary, who he now thought of as a right Irish bitch. But all that was over, he had been accepted by the gentry and because he had the added title of Lord, he reigned supreme; it gave him more power!

Charles hired two new staff, a cook-cum-housekeeper and a gardener. He wanted the estate to look as beautiful as it had always done when his mother cared for it. She was the added beauty, but Charles couldn't find it in his heart to acknowledge this. But then he didn't have a warm heart; his was made of stone. He had to be addressed by the staff as Lord Charles. This gave him a feeling of superiority and importance, something within his own mind he rightfully deserved. Under his ownership the estate would revert back to old English formalities where the commoners were ruled by the aristocracy. Charles was in his element, this was the very life he yearned for.

He spent most of the day running his law practice, as clients were flocking to him because of his sign outside the office. It read: 'Lord Charles Rothchild, Qualified Lawyer and Estate Owner'. The English were proud of their peerage. His Irish land ownership had been reduced from eighteen farms to eight, but his law business was able to prop up any shortfalls that might occur. The other gentry owners were not so lucky, as they only had their Irish lands to keep them in the lifestyle they were accustomed to. It was time to call a meeting at Lord Charles's estate. The wheat crop had been harvested and now was ready to be brought across the Irish Sea to England to be sold. But of course, this year they didn't have the same bargaining power as previous years; they were ten farms fewer, those being the ones taken from Lord Charles's estate by his mother, Mary. The wheat from these ten farms was remaining in Ireland for the Irish people. How was this going to affect the English estate owners? One of the owners was in talks with a wheat importer and he was told 'things looked bleak indeed'. Price rises were imminent, thus why the meeting had to be called. This was the first meeting since Mary had left, so Charles was in full control. He wanted to show his dominance by the fact he was a lord, so everything had to run to schedule and on time. The cook and the butler would attend to after-meeting drinks and hors d'oeuvres; they knew their positions and what was expected of them.

As the carriages rolled up, the gardener was there to tether the horses to a hitching rail at the stables, where he would feed and water them. This, of course, had been Connor's job, but no longer. Charles stood in all pomp and ceremony as he greeted the gentry as they walked into the boardroom. This was an important meeting as it hinged on the livelihood of all the estate owners. Lord Charles welcomed everyone and the meeting commenced. First on the agenda to discuss was the cost to import the wheat across the Irish Sea to England. The Irish wharf workers were demanding more pay and threatened to strike if this was not forthcoming. This, the English had no control over, as it was an Irish problem and had to be sorted on that side. Now they were going to be held to ransom if this was not solved within a short period of time, as their wheat had to remain in Ireland, for how long? they wondered. Because of Mary's cause and the farms she now owned, there was no need for the Irish to buy wheat from the English, as they now had their own source. So, the English estate owners' wheat would sit in the clearing sheds until it was passed for export if the strike went ahead. These were nervous times. This was a huge worry to the gentry, as they needed their wheat money to keep their estates running, but they were at the mercy of the Irish wharf workers now.

Had the tide turned, was this time for the Irish to punish the English, to give them a snippet on how life could be if problems arose that they had no control over? God knows how they had suffered, for so little as a small piece of bread to stop them from starving. All the English would miss was their lavish lifestyles; starvation was never a word that entered their minds, nor probably was in their vocabulary. These words only related to the poor who had experienced such horrors. Someone brought up Mary's name, and now the blame lay squarely on her shoulders. "If Mary hadn't taken away the bulk of the Rothchild farms, and we have to end up selling our wheat in Ireland, she would surely undercut us. The Irish would see fit to buy her wheat before ours. Where does this leave us, gentlemen?" he asked. Silence befell the meeting. "We will have no choice but to raise our land tariffs to the tenant farmers if the export prices rise," replied another farmer. Never had there been such a disappointed lot of men, thus causing the meeting to end on a sour note. Another meeting was called for in a fortnight's time to assess what was happening with the waterfront saga. If Mary had been a fly on the wall, she would have been amused.

The men adjourned to the drawing room for their usual drinks and hors d'oeuvres. It was not the same without their beautiful Mary, but no-one made mention of this although it remained tucked up in their individual minds. She had completely captured Lord Albert's heart and if they were truthful to themselves, they were hugely jealous. Now, of course, there was talk among the gentry to see who could palm their daughter on to Lord Charles; what a catch, he had it all. To have a lord as part of the family, their daughter would then become Lady Rothchild. This was the wish of every estate owner.

But no-one knew about Charles's secret life. This, of course, could never be revealed, as he would be shunned by the upper class and perhaps lose his clientele at his law office. George would be known solely as Lord Charles's personal butler. Their dark secret would be kept between themselves; although two other people knew: Rose, his half-sister; and a friend of Charles's, who left a letter under the pillow addressed to her, but who? Would he share the secret with anyone else? He had shared it with her, but this Lord Charles knew nothing about. One thing for sure, she would never tell anyone as she was so ashamed. It would never pass her lips, not even her husband knew. This would bring such shame to the family. Charles she didn't care about, but her mother would never forgive herself for bringing such a child into this world; the blame would be on her conscience forever, she could never live with this truth.

Now that George had cleaned up after the gentry he went to the privacy of his and Lord Charles's wing and poured two glasses of wine, one for Lord Charles and one for himself. The housemaid was only allowed to enter their wing of the mansion on a Monday to clean, other than that it was out of bounds. This was not uncommon in upper-class households; there were boundaries and strict rules to be obeyed by the staff. This was the men's love-nest. George had been smitten by Lord Charles and couldn't believe his luck when asked to be his personal butler on the beautiful Rothchild estate. They had met at college where George was the gardener and Lord Charles was an upper-class student. Every time their paths crossed something strange happened inside of Lord Charles; here was a strong, handsome young man, partially stripped as he went about his gardening chores. His tanned skin and his protruding muscles excited him. He was forever on Lord Charles's mind, hence the invitation for him to come and live on his estate with him. He had tried to date the opposite sex but he soon tired of them, or they tired of him and his selfish and arrogant manner towards them. Where did this mannerism come from? His father, Lord Albert, was a gentle man with feelings; did Charles take after his grandfather? He certainly didn't inherit his mother's nature, she was a beautiful lady! After seeing the last gentry off he made his way to his wing where he knew his lover would be waiting with a glass of wine. They discussed the meeting, which had left everyone a bit flat, and now it was a waiting game to see if the wharf workers went ahead with their strike. George had a question for Lord Charles: "The men were discussing whose daughter would be suitable for you. Where does this leave me?" "Don't worry, George, women are not for me," he told him with the utmost confidence.

Two weeks had passed and yes, the Irish wharf workers had gone on strike. Ireland was recovering from the potato famine and money was scarce, people were still suffering in the business sector. The wharf workers refused to load the wheat bound for England in sympathy with the tenant farmers who like themselves were struggling to make a living. Especially when the wheat was grown in Ireland just to supply the English. English absentee ownership was a blight on Ireland. They weren't interested in the plight of the Irish.

Today was the day of the next boardroom meeting with the gentry. Most of the gentry were reliant on their wheat money to keep their estates afloat, as this was their main income, other than the land tariffs paid to them by their tenant farmers. But the money from the wheat yield was needed most. The news was grim; no wheat was going to be handled in the foreseeable future, thus meaning it would sit in the loading sheds indefinitely. If it got damp it would start to shoot in the sacks, and this spelt ruin. This had never happened before, so the estate owners were up in arms, but they could do nothing. Now a little pain was being inflicted upon them and this didn't go down at all well. If only they could have imagined the unbearable pain the Irish suffered, then they might have shown a little compassion for them. There was no solution, they were at a stalemate; all there was left to do was to wait. In the meantime, several of the gentry would have to pull rank with their banks and ask for a loan to see them through. "Now let us make a decision on the possibility of raising our land tariffs," said Lord Charles. "We will take a vote." Of course, everyone was in agreeance, but what of the poor tenant farmer? He was Irish; did it really matter?

Mary's English solicitor had heard of the estate owners' plight, so he wrote her a letter explaining the dilemma that was facing them. There was even some mention of some of the Irish farms having to be sold so they could keep their estates. Would she be interested in purchasing any if they came up for sale? If so, he would act on her behalf as a silent bidder; then no-one would know who was showing interest. If they had any suspicion it was Mary, they would never agree to sell to her. He knew she could well and truly afford them, besides if she could help more Irish tenant farmers, that spelt sweet revenge! He would eagerly await her reply.

Several months had passed and still the wheat sat in the store sheds in Ireland. Tonight, one of the wealthier estate owners was putting on an evening and had invited Lord Charles as a guest. He had a daughter and he was looking for a husband for her. Who could be more eligible than Lord Charles? He didn't seem to have a lady friend, perhaps his daughter would be suitable. She had been schooled up on how to treat the gentry. The thought of any one of their daughters becoming Lady Rothchild was on all their minds, but who would he choose? Some of the daughters were beautiful, some were not so beautiful. This was the sole purpose of this evening, to introduce his daughter to Lord Charles. The wife had cooked a lovely supper so they all sat around the dining table enjoying the food and drinking wine. The daughter was very attentive towards Lord Charles and he felt quite flattered by this. He was the focal point and he felt comfortable in this position. "You don't have a permanent lady friend, Lord Charles?" asked Elizabeth's father. "No, I am unattached at the moment, I am in no hurry to settle down. My law practice is going well and my tenant farms will hopefully make me plenty of money. One day I may want to settle down but not at the moment." The father looked at his daughter with disappointment; he had hoped for a better outcome. The evening passed pleasantly but with no end result. As Lord Charles bid his hosts goodnight, Elizabeth walked him to the door and thanked him for his company. She stood on her toes and gently kissed him on the cheek. He was startled by this act of kindness, as he saw it. To her this was an invitation for him to make an advance towards her, but this did not happen. He tipped his hat as he bade her goodnight. When she returned to the drawing room her father spoke his piece: "He's a good catch. You could have a wonderful life with Lord Charles and become Lady Rothchild and live in that beautiful mansion. Try harder next time, girl!"

These words echoed in Elizabeth's mind. What did she have to do to get his attention? Perhaps she could ride up to the mansion and call on him! She loved horses and rode like a champion. Yes, that's what she could do, pay him a visit and challenge him to a race, but it would have to be at the weekend as he was at his office most of the week. She would spend the week brushing up on her horse-riding skills, perhaps even a little bare-back riding would make him notice her.

Saturday morning had arrived and Elizabeth pulled on her riding jodhpurs and a sexy silk top, leaving the top buttons undone to show off a little bare flesh. She jumped on her horse and rode skilfully towards the mansion. As she neared the building she saw a man standing at the front entrance. She rode up to him and asked, "Is Lord Charles at home?" This was George, who was taken by surprise. What was a female doing asking after his lover? With this, Lord Charles appeared. "Hi, I thought we might go for a ride. I enjoyed your company on Wednesday night," said Elizabeth. "Wait and I will saddle up," he yelled as he made way to his stables. He felt smug. I will show her a thing or two, he thought to himself. Meanwhile George was seething inside, he felt hurt. Who was she and what did she mean when she said she enjoyed his company the other night? Was he being double-crossed? Lord Charles said he was going out, he didn't say it was to her place.

Lord Charles walked his horse over and climbed into the saddle. "Come, we will do a round of the paddock," he called as he took off. Elizabeth kicked her horse into gear and away they went flat tack. It didn't take long for her to catch and overtake him, being the first to reach the gate. He was hurt, never before had he been beaten, let alone by a female. "Let's go for a canter through the woods," he suggested. Away they went. He then set a course for them to race on; he had to prove himself, so the race began. Elizabeth decided to fake a fall in the thicket, perhaps then she could make a play for him. She saw him ride into the distance and when he reached the end, he was so pleased with himself, as she was not in sight. But as time went on and Elizabeth had not turned up, he started to worry, so he retraced his steps. He came across her horse but no Elizabeth. What had happened? He called out to her but to no avail. As he made his way back through the woods, there she lay holding on to her ankle. "Are you all right?" he asked. "I fell off my horse, I think I have done something to my ankle." "Let me have a look," so she rolled up her jodhpurs. He took hold of her leg. "It looks fine, perhaps you have just sprained it," he said. "I will carry you back to my home and you can rest it for a while." She thanked him as he lifted her into his arms. She had managed to undo another button so to expose her breasts a little more to him. As he carried her back, his gaze fell upon her bare skin. Never before had he seen such rounded breasts, not that he had ever taken notice of these features before on any female, but now that they were in front of him he felt something. He had no interest in the opposite sex, so he thought, but why did he look at these features on Elizabeth? She smiled at him sweetly; perhaps this could be the beginning of something between them? He called to the horses and they followed them out of the woods.

George looked up to see Lord Charles carrying the young lady in his arms. He felt jealous but he could not let his feelings be known in public; he would have his say later. Elizabeth was placed on the settee to rest her ankle. George offered to make her a cup of tea, which she graciously accepted, while Lord Charles went and tethered the horses. Her gaze was capturing the beautiful surroundings. The drawing room was tastefully furnished, but of course this had been chosen by Lord Charles's mother, when she lived here. Could all this be hers one day? If so, how wonderful. This would indeed please her father, his daughter as Lady Rothchild; it would lift their standing among the upper class. After Elizabeth had rested for an hour, Lord Charles helped her to her horse. She thanked him, then took her leave and rode quietly down the road, with hope in her heart that this was going to advance into a lustful relationship.

It took another three months before the gentry's wheat was loaded onto the ship to cross the Irish Sea. The landowners were worried as to what condition it would arrive in. Had it been stored at the right temperature while sitting in the storage sheds waiting to be loaded onto the ship? Several of the men were in debt to the bank, so were desperate to sell their yield. Grains become biologically active and respire if they are not stored properly, thus encouraging fungal and insect problems along with germination, rendering it unmarketable. This was in the back of their minds. Several of the gentry made the journey down to London to the wharf to check that the wheat had arrived in good condition. But to their horror, it was sprouting through the sacks, thus their worst fears were realised, for they had nothing to sell. Never before had they faced such a dilemma. How were they going to survive? Even with an increase in their tenant farmers' tariffs it was not enough to see them through to next season. This spelt disaster and the only way ahead for several of the men was to sell off a farm thus reducing their holdings.

Mary's solicitor had heard back from her and yes, she was definitely interested in buying back any Irish farms that were coming up for sale. This meant she could look after more Irish farmers and make life a little easier for them. To take the land from the greedy English landowners was her dearest wish. Anything that would help restore faith for her people, as the lands had been taken from them by the then King of England, King John, and given to his knights and followers. She felt deeply for the Irish; now it was time to look after her fellow countrymen who had put up with years of suffering. She would let her solicitor act on her behalf and handle any sales, as the gentry would never sell to Mary; this meant it would go back to the Irish, and this they did not want. All trace of the Irish had vanished when Mary and her family walked away from the Rothchild estate, taking with them the red Irish hair.

Lord Charles was better off than his fellow estate owners, as his law firm was thriving. It would keep him afloat, but three other owners were going to be forced to reduce their holdings by selling one of their Irish farms. They hoped after next year's wheat yield they would be able to buy them back. Lord Charles would have liked to have bought them but he didn't want to over-commit. He wouldn't take the risk. Mary's solicitor put in a bid to buy the three farms on behalf of a silent client. The offer was fair so they reluctantly accepted, mentioning they would like to buy them back on the results of a good wheat yield next season. The solicitor couldn't promise anything, but he would make mention of these wishes to his client, knowing full well they would never again belong to the English. They would have been horrified if they knew the farms now belonged to Mary. This gave them less bargaining power when importing back to England next season, but this they didn't know. They naturally thought the new buyer would be an English gentleman so the same volume would be coming back across the Irish Sea.

Lord Charles's relationship with George was still going strong, although there was another player on the scene, which did leave George a little miffed. But as was explained by Lord Charles, he had to be seen to show a little interest in the opposite sex, so as to keep any gossip at bay. Often Lord Charles would go riding with Elizabeth; he was always trying to outdo her, but she was just as competitive as he. She could see that if their relationship was to flourish, she would have to give in to his wish to outride her. She had all the encouragement of her family, especially her father; what a feather in his cap if his daughter was to became Lady Rothchild. Many other ladies were making themselves available encouraged by their fathers, but Elizabeth seemed to be Lord Charles's choice at the moment. Of course, this was the cover-up needed to hide his secret life.

Gossip was rife among the estate owners. Who was the new landowner? Who had purchased the three farms? Did he live in the district? Was he of gentry standing? Mary's solicitor was asked to attend the next board meeting held at the Rothchild estate, as they hoped he would reveal the silent buyer; he must be of high standing to afford to buy three farms. The meeting was arranged for the following Thursday and an invite was extended to the new owner to attend with the solicitor. Would Mary front up or remain anonymous? Of course, she wanted to remain silent as her last memories of the estate were not happy ones. She had never forgiven Charles for his outward display of hatred for the Irish. This even extended to his half brothers and sister. He had completely divorced himself from the fact he was part Irish and that he had his mother's blood running through his veins as well as his English heritage. He couldn't stand the fact that Irish blood produced red hair, and he was happy when all those with red hair left with his mother.

The day of the meeting had arrived and the gentry were anxious to know who the land had been sold to. Who was the mystery gentleman? Would he be attending the meeting? They all assembled in the boardroom but there wasn't a stranger among them. As Lord Charles began chairing the meeting, in walked the local solicitor, but he was on his own. He was welcomed and asked to sit at the main table so he could answer any questions asked of him. Within minutes the questions started. Who was the mystery buyer? "The buyer does not want to be identified. I have just found out it was bought by an Irish bidder," he told the meeting. A deadly silence befell the boardroom; an Irish owner, they did not want to hear this. "Does he live in England?" someone asked. "No, they reside in

Ireland," replied the solicitor. "Will we be able to buy our land back if we have a good season?" one asked. "I'm sorry, gentlemen, I have no answer for you on that, but I did put in the contract it must be offered back to the original owners if it went up for sale. Other than that, I cannot volunteer any further information, so I will take my leave and let you carry on with your meeting. Good day, gentlemen." With this he excused himself and left. Again, the room fell silent as they worked out in their minds what this meant, what consequences would befall them. "What if the wheat was to stay in Ireland? Our import quota will be reduced significantly, this will hurt us," said a concerned owner. Suddenly a dreadful thought came to Lord Charles: what if his mother was the silent owner? This would give her thirteen farms, and she would be the largest landowner. This would mean the wheat would definitely not be crossing the Irish Sea. Would he keep this thought to himself or share it with the gentry? But before he could make his decision there was a sudden outburst. "What if it was Lord Albert's Mary? We will never see our lands again, we are doomed," said one of the farmers that had sold off a farm. Lord Charles was devastated. Even though his family had left England they still haunted him, if this was indeed true? He had no contact with them, he knew nothing of their whereabouts. He had to regain his composure and continue chairing the meeting. "Now we have to deal with the problem of our wasted wheat, what are we going to do? Perhaps it could be used as stock food, this we must look into."

The meeting ended on a low as everyone had the same thoughts. Was this their arch rival Mary who had betrayed them and bought their land? Even through this murky haze, they still remembered her for her beauty, this would never be forgotten. Lord Charles couldn't wait for the meeting to end, he wanted rid of everybody, as he needed time to himself. He was livid to think his mother, of all people, could have scored more land, if indeed she was the buyer. If he had thought for one minute they would end up in Irish hands, he would have bought them himself. But now it was too late! He felt betrayed and once again was beaten at his own game.

George was waiting for his lover to come and have his customary after-meeting drink, but he did not arrive. He went in search of him and found him sobbing like a child in the boardroom. "Come, Lord Charles, what is wrong?" he wanted to know. "Go away, George, I want to be on my own," he fired back. George went to comfort him, but his actions met with rebuff. He knew then it was time to make himself scarce, his master was in one of his petulant moods. He made his way back to their wing and decided that the spare glass of wine would not be wasted. What was the night going to bring?

Lord Charles did not want any of George's pity tonight, so he decided to take the carriage into town. As he was nearing Elizabeth's father's estate he made a spur-of-the-moment decision and turned into their driveway. He tethered the horses in the stables and walked over to the front entrance, then rang the doorbell. The door opened and there was Elizabeth. "Why hello, Lord Charles, this is a pleasant surprise, do come in." She led him into the drawing room and asked him to be seated. Elizabeth could see he was brooding, she had seen it many times before, with her own father. "May I pour you a whisky?" she enquired. "That would be nice, thank you." She could see he wasn't in a talkative mood so went over and sat at the piano, then started to play. Lord Charles closed his eyes and listened to the music. It was soothing after his disappointing day, and he felt relaxed. His black mood was slowly subsiding only to be completely forgotten when Elizabeth burst into song. She had a beautiful voice. He walked over and poured himself another whisky, as he didn't want to interrupt her. She could see he was enjoying himself so she kept on playing and he kept on drinking. Elizabeth decided to seize on this opportunity; her mind was working overtime as she could still hear her father's voice, 'Try harder next time'. Was this the time?

Her parents had been invited to some friends' place for the evening, so she and Lord Charles were home alone. She looked at him; his eyes were barely open, he seemed totally relaxed, so she went over to him and coaxed him off his chair, then took his hand and led him to her bedroom. She sat him on her bed then proceeded to undress. Her clothes fell in a pile on the floor. Suddenly, there before him stood Elizabeth, totally naked. He had never seen a naked lady before, her skin looked so soft and delicate, not at all like George's which was tanned and tough. His eyes perused her body, which left him stunned, as she was actually quite beautiful to look at. Elizabeth came over and unbuttoned his jacket and put her hands inside his shirt and caressed his chest, slowly moving her hands down to his waist. Then he felt his belt being unbuckled and his trousers being pulled from his body. He panicked, he wanted to pull them up again, but it was all too late. Her hands were touching his personal parts playing with them. It was now or never. She had to act, if she was to become Lady Rothchild and please her father, now was the time. She climbed on the bed beside him and pushed her body into his, but he just lay there, so she caressed his lower body, which was limp. What was wrong? Perhaps the alcohol had affected him, nothing was happening! She took his hand and put it on her feminine parts coaxing him to play with her, still nothing was moving down below so she nibbled at his ear whispering naughty words trying to excite him. Suddenly there was action and he sprung to life, the bed started to shake, Lord Charles was like a caged lion that had just been let loose. He was rough; never had she experienced such behaviour before. It left her feeling a little afraid, but all she could think of was her father's words, 'Try harder next time'. Now Elizabeth was not the innocent young lady that her father believed she was; she had taken several lovers, so she was no virgin. Only she knew this. She did wonder if Lord Charles was a virgin. Was this his first time with a lady, as his bedside manners were those of someone unfamiliar with pleasing a woman?

When Lord Charles woke next morning he was surprised. Where was he? This certainly was not his and George's bedroom. He sat up and there was Elizabeth lying naked beside him. Then it all came flooding back. "Wake up, Elizabeth, I have to leave before your father finds us together." With this she stirred and realised the full implications that confronted them. This was not the behaviour that happened in upper-class circles. They both dressed quickly, then she opened the bedroom door to see if the way was clear. Just as Lord Charles was creeping down the hallway he heard a voice: "Just a minute, young man, where the hell do you think you are going?" and there stood Elizabeth's father. "Oh, it's you, Lord Charles. If you have bedded my daughter, the best thing you can do is make an honest woman of her. She is damaged goods now, no-one will want her. Think about this," he said as he let him out the front door. Poor Lord Charles, he had been caught, there was no way out. He was a victim of circumstances, but his own petulant behaviour had led to this. Now he would have to marry Elizabeth.

He untethered his horses and climbed up on the carriage. Where to now? He couldn't go back to the estate. What was he going to tell George? He decided to head to his office where he could sit and think of what was going to follow. He had dishonoured his fellow estate owner's daughter, such shame it would bring to their family. Of course, now he would have to do the honourable deed and ask for her hand in marriage. There was no way out of this situation. But as he sat and thought about the night, it was Elizabeth that had led him on. If she was out to get him, she had succeeded, and now he was trapped. How was he going to break this to George? He was the only person he had been in a relationship with, until last night. He loved George, what the hell was he doing with Elizabeth? But if he wanted an heir to pass his title and estate on to, then he had to take a wife, as George wasn't going to do the trick, He could still be his lover though? It would just mean there would be three people in this relationship, as he wasn't prepared to give George up for Elizabeth or any other woman for that matter. He would have them both. Elizabeth would be the camouflage for their dark secret.

His mind went back to yesterday's meeting. So much had happened since then. He was caught up in the presumption that it was his mother, Mary, who was the new owner of the three farms, especially when he had heard it was an Irish buyer. This was the cause of his letting his guard down and being swept away in Elizabeth's sweet music. This, mixed with a few whiskies, led to that fateful decision to bed her. Did he really feel anything for her? It had all happened so quickly, he didn't really know. He had to admit he liked listening to her play the piano and singing. Perhaps to have this in his mansion would be acceptable. He had to find some positives. But what of George?

Meanwhile George was worried about Lord Charles, as he had left in a petulant mood. Where had he gone? He didn't come home last night to their bed. George lay awake most of the night worrying about him. This morning he was still alone. He dressed and walked to the stables to see if the carriage was there, but alas, it was not. Where would he have spent the night? Sometimes Lord Charles's manner left a lot to be desired, but George only found this out when he came to live on the estate. He could overlook this, as his feelings for him ruled his heart. Where else could he live on such a beautiful estate? His lifestyle was that of a kept man, and he had Lord Charles all to himself! This he felt safe about, because their dark secret could never be revealed. It would cost Lord Charles dearly, and his title meant more to him than any other possession.

Later in the morning George saw the carriage being driven up the driveway, so he walked into the drawing room to wait for him. It was no use attacking him, this would only make matters worse; he was the spoilt boy, no-one questioned him, he was his own person. As he entered, George could see he was agitated so offered to make him a cup of tea, but instead he asked for a whisky. He poured him one and sat on the settee next to him, neither speaking a word. Just as Lord Charles was about to speak, the doorbell rang, so George left to answer it. "Lord Charles, Mr Barnaby is here to see you," he announced. He could see Lord Charles stiffen up at the announcement of this name. Why? This was only Elizabeth's father. "I would like to speak to you in private, Lord Charles," he said and waved his hand for George to be dismissed from this conversation. George left, he was only a servant to the outside world. This annoyed him as it made him feel second class. He closed the door and lingered on the other side, just in case he was needed. He felt uneasy about Mr Barnaby's manner, he seemed a little agitated. "Right, Lord Charles, let us get this out in the open. I expect you to make an honest lady of my daughter. What you did was ruin her reputation, now you must do the right thing by her. You have my blessing to marry her. This calls for a drink." Lord Charles poured them both a whisky and they raised their glasses. He quietly applauded his daughter, as now his dearest wish had been granted, and she was about to become Lady Rothchild, what a boost to their name.

On the other side of the door stood a shocked man, one who was so upset he ran to their room in tears. He had been betrayed! Lord Charles had spent last night in Elizabeth's bed instead of in their bed with him. He didn't think his lover liked women. Was he bisexual? There had been no mention of this, ever! He always portrayed them as second-class citizens, he even treated his mother and sister with contempt. Why was Elizabeth different? Did he love her? So many questions were running through his head, but there were no answers to any of them. He climbed under the duvet cover and sobbed like a lost child. Was this the end of his days at the Rothchild estate?

The discussion and celebrations went on for several hours between Lord Charles and Mr Barnaby. One whisky bottle was emptied and another one opened. There seemed to be no animosity between these two men, for which Lord Charles was very thankful. He promised he would propose to Elizabeth at a dinner at the Barnaby home next Friday. The two men shook hands and Mr Barnaby took his leave, although none too steady on his feet. He climbed onto the carriage with much difficulty, then whipped the horses to get going. As he was driving home he was overexcited about his Elizabeth and Lord Charles, so yelled at the horses to go faster. They took fright and swerved, throwing him into a ditch on the side of the road. He lay there dreaming about handing his daughter to another household, the most important one at that, then a darkness descended, and all his wonderful thoughts disappeared.

Lord Charles had enough Dutch courage to face George. Where was he? He made his way to their bedroom where he found George huddled under the bedclothes in a right old state. "What's wrong, George?" "You tell me. Where were you last night?" he sobbed. He had to think quickly. George seemed upset so he decided not to tell him the truth. "I was upset, I spent the night at the office." He would tell the truth when he lay with him in bed. This was the final straw. George jumped out of bed, dressed and left the home. The carriage was still attached to the horses so he climbed aboard and away he went. As he drove down the road a bit he could see two horses galloping at top speed with no-one on the carriage to steer them. That's strange, he thought. He whipped his horses to try to catch up with the uncontrolled carriage and it wasn't until several hundred yards that he managed to stop them. He reached for their reins and pulled the horses up. Where was the driver? Who did they belong to? He jumped down and tethered the horses and carriage to the back of his carriage and continued on to the next estate. Perhaps they would know who they belonged to. As he turned into the driveway he could see someone at the stables, and when he got closer he saw it was Elizabeth. He called out to her and she came over. "What are you doing with father's carriage?" she asked. "I found it unattended on the road, the horses were running wild." "Where's father?" she questioned. Suddenly it dawned on George that something must have happen to him after he left the Rothchild estate. "Come, we must find your father, he must have fallen from the carriage after he visited Lord Charles." "What do you mean, was he at the Rothchild estate?" she asked. "Yes, he seemed angry when he asked to talk to Lord Charles." Elizabeth knew immediately what the conversation would have been about.

"Why would he be angry with Lord Charles?" asked George, hoping for more information about last night. "Because he slept over and father caught him leaving my room. He has demanded that he make an honest woman of me, which he hopefully has promised to do. Soon I will be Lady Rothchild," she announced proudly. Then her thoughts went back to her father. "But what of father, where is he?" "Let us retrace back to the estate and see if we can find him," suggested George. Now he had the news straight from the horse's mouth; Lord Charles could no longer lie of his whereabouts last night. Elizabeth sat beside George on the carriage as they searched the roadside for her father. It wasn't long before they spotted something lying in a ditch. They pulled up and there was Mr Barnaby. Poor Elizabeth, she called to him but there was no answer. She and George dismounted and went to his assistance, to see if he was still breathing, and all they could smell was alcohol. He was unconscious so they loaded him into the carriage and drove him to the hospital. He was taken to a ward but there would be no information on him for quite some time, as they had to wait for a doctor. George then took Elizabeth back to their home so she could tell her family what had happened. He decided to carry on back to the Rothchild estate as he had calmed down a little, but there would be questions asked!

Lord Charles was frantic; where had George gone? One minute he was lying distraught in the bed, next thing he was nowhere to be seen. He had searched everywhere for him, several hours had past and still no George. He walked to the front entrance again and he saw him coming up the driveway with the carriage. He waited until he was within hearing range and called to him, "Where have you been, George? I've looked all over the estate for you." George tethered the horses and came over to him. "I have just delivered your future father-in-law to the hospital." "What do you mean?" he asked. "You have some explaining to do, I want the truth this time," said an angry George. Lord Charles leaned over and asked him to come to their wing, as he didn't want to be overheard by the gardener or the cook.

They sat on their bed and he explained to George what had happened. How Elizabeth had taken advantage of him as he had had too many whiskies, and that combined with overload from the meeting was a lethal cocktail. "But George, this makes no difference to our lives, we can still be lovers. I will set rules for Elizabeth, she will never enter our wing. This will be out of bounds to her, this is our private area. Besides, this is the cover-up we need." Now it was time for George to tell what had happened to Mr Barnaby, that he had fallen from his carriage and was in hospital, and as yet no-one knew the extent of his injuries. Lord Charles felt responsible as they had polished off two bottles of whisky.

A day had passed when Elizabeth rode to the Rothchild estate to say the dinner was off on Friday, as her father had ended up with a broken leg and would be in hospital for a couple of weeks. Today Lord Charles was still recovering from his overdose on whisky. He hadn't made it to work so had taken the day off. "I'm sorry about your father, Elizabeth, perhaps I should have asked George to drive him home. We did have a few whiskies, just a premature celebration." "Father was not happy about the fall, but he is happy about our pending engagement. We just have to put it off for a few weeks until he gets out of hospital. He has requested this," said Elizabeth. With this she came over and gave Lord Charles a kiss on his cheek. "I can't wait for our engagement party, I'm so happy." There was very little input from Lord Charles, as he still felt he had been cheated.

2

The Engagement Party

The big night had arrived. All the estate owners and the who's who of the area were invited. Mr Barnaby was feeling very perky, as he could now lay claim to his Elizabeth becoming Lady Rothchild. This he had had on his mind for several years and now that his daughter had snared Lord Charles, he could hold himself in high esteem! To have a lord as part of the family was indeed honourable. The eldest son born to Elizabeth would one day take over his father's lordship and become heir to the Rothchild estate. The party was under way and everyone was having a good time, but sadly George, Lord Charles's butler, had not been invited, as this was for the upper class, not for servants. He felt hurt about being bypassed, he was just as important as Elizabeth; they were both Lord Charles's lovers!

Elizabeth looked beautiful in her expensive dress, a present from her father. She had to be the belle of the night. All the other landowners' daughters were disappointed that Lord Charles had settled for someone other than themselves. Mr Barnaby had gone to a lot of expense to have everything perfect for this special night. Lord Charles was inundated with congratulations on his choice of a bride. But Mrs Barnaby was not so happy as she had a bad feeling about Lord Charles; she found him to be cold and calculating. She had seen the way he had treated his family, especially his siblings, and she did remember hearing about an incident when they lost their eldest son. She worried what lay in store for her daughter, but being a woman, her thoughts were overridden by the male ego. She was on her third wine and was trying to put these ugly thoughts out of her mind. She knew from experience a woman's say amounted to very little in the gentry households, they were mere chattels. "Oh goodness, my glass is empty," she said out loud so someone fetched her another. She was tired of everyone telling her what a wonderful catch Lord Charles was. She had tried to talk to Elizabeth about her feelings on Lord Charles, but she was blinded by all the glitz and glamour that the Rothchild estate would afford her. She was the envy of all the young ladies in the area. Whereas Mr Barnaby walked around with his chest puffed out like a peacock, he was so proud of Elizabeth's choice of a husband. He had no idea his daughter was not the pure young lady he thought she was. Lord Charles had not picked up on this the night he bedded her, because of the state of mind he was in.

The party was coming to an end, so Mr Barnaby was

ready to make his speech. He asked for his wife to come and stand beside him, and as she staggered her way over, Elizabeth came to the rescue and whipped her off to her bedroom. She didn't want to be embarrassed, as this was a most important occasion, and Lord Charles did not need to see this. There was to be no distractions away from her tonight. She lay her mother on her bed and pulled a cover over her, then went back to listen to the rest of her father's speech. It was all about him and how proud he was, that these two prominent families were going to be united. He hoped there would be the 'pitter patter' of little feet on the Rothchild estate once they were married. Elizabeth felt embarrassed as she thought that was a long way off, a very long way off! She still felt Lord Charles had been a virgin until their night together. His actions were far from a display of affection, more of aggression, which she hoped would change. It was now time for Lord Charles to announce his engagement to Elizabeth. "Will you accept this engagement ring, Elizabeth?" and he put the ring on her finger. She reached up and kissed him and he took her hand, then they mingled with all the guests.

When Lord Charles returned to the estate after the party, he found George out to it on the settee in the drawing room, with an empty bottle of whisky lying on the carpet. He had been having a little party of his own. The thought of all the glitz and glamour at the neighbouring estate was just too much for him to handle, he was being pushed aside, and this hurt him deep down to the very core of his heart. Very soon he would have to share Lord Charles with Elizabeth, and with this thought in mind, he drank to his sorrow! Lord Charles fetched a blanket and lay it over George. He was ready for bed, the night had been too much, he just wanted to escape all thoughts of the Barnaby family.

3

Married Life

Lord Charles wanted the wedding to be held before the wheat harvesting arrived, in case there were any more problems arising with the importation of the wheat. Most of the gentry had managed to survive last season's disaster, but some had to cut their cloth to suit their reduced incomes. It was indeed a lean year for most, so there were high hopes of a bumper yield this coming season, in fact they were relying on it! Still no-one had found out who the silent buyer was that had purchased the three farms, but if all went well this season, they would buy them back.

The wedding was to take place tomorrow, so the town was abuzz for this high-society event. It was decided to hold the reception in the gardens on the Rothchild estate, this way George could be part of the celebrations. He along with the gardener had worked hard to spruce up the gardens to have them looking stunning. The marquees had been set up and it all looked picture perfect.

Everybody had left, just Lord Charles and George remained. George took his lover in his arms and whirled him around the marquee. This was going to be their night to celebrate, because tomorrow he would lie in Elizabeth's bed and in her arms. This thought brought tears to his eyes, for tomorrow he had to share him with another. But this moment was theirs. They danced together and held each other close, making a promise that nothing would change in their lives, their love for each other would remain strong and binding.

Lord Charles was feeling nervous today, as he wasn't used to being organised by other parties; he was his own person, and he had been all his life. The only noticeable thing missing was his family: not one member was there to share this special day, because no-one had been invited. The Irish heritage was gone, it was no longer part of his life. It finished when they walked off the estate, the red hair was gone forever. The Irish curse had left him. He had bought a lovely wedding present for Elizabeth, a piano, and now it held pride of place in the drawing room. She would be able to play and sing for him and George. Perhaps he would get her to play it tonight, so as to relax him before he bedded her. He was petrified as to how it would all pan out! Elizabeth's wing in the mansion was all organised; it was not unusual for men to have their own private wing. After all, this was the British aristocracy!

Arrangements were made where the marital duties would be performed and Lord Charles chose for these to take place in Elizabeth's bedroom. He would visit her when he wanted, but she was never to come to his wing. This he had made very clear to her, for reasons only he and George knew. Lord Charles and Elizabeth had not bedded each other since that night at Elizabeth's home, so she was hoping for a better outcome tonight. She was excited as she knew what it was like to be loved by a man; she had experienced the pleasures from a couple of previous encounters. Not that anyone but herself knew! Lord Charles didn't seem to pick up on the fact that she wasn't a virgin, but then he was pretty overcome with whisky when she lured him into her bed. Tonight was going to be wonderful, in her own bed at the Rothchild mansion.

All the guests were seated in the marquee, the groom and groomsmen were waiting for the bride to arrive in her horsedrawn carriage, accompanied by her proud father. Mrs Barnaby was seated between her two sons, who were her minders today; no-one wanted a repeat performance of what happened at the engagement party. Lord Charles looked a million dollars in his wedding attire but deep down he was not excited. In fact, if he didn't have to think to the future for an heir to his estate, this day would not be happening. He was happy with George. The bride's carriage had arrived and out climbed Mr Barnaby, who reached to help his daughter dismount from the carriage. She looked radiant in her beautiful wedding gown. Her bridesmaids held her train until they reached the grass, then it was left to flow. Mr Barnaby took Elizabeth's arm in his and walked her down the aisle to the waiting groom. This was his proudest moment, all eyes were upon him; in a few minutes the two families would be joined by marriage. Lord Charles watched his bride walk towards him; he had to admit she looked lovely today but this did not mean his feelings were any more for her. She would give him the son he wanted, as well as be the camouflage for his dark secret. All he had to do was visit her bedroom occasionally, perform his marital duties, it was as simple as that ... or not!

Once the nuptials were over, the bride and groom walked among their guests accepting all the compliments and best wishes that were being bestowed upon them. Elizabeth clung to her husband's arm, he was hers now, they were Lord and Lady Rothchild. He was not used to having someone so close to him, let alone hanging off his arm; he felt controlled. This did not sit comfortably with him, but today he had to go along with protocol. Tomorrow would be different, things would be on his terms from that day forth! But today belonged to Elizabeth. Celebrations went on well into the night with everyone enjoying themselves, except for one person, who watched on with such jealous rage in his eyes. He felt belittled as a servant, and due to his closeness to Lord Charles, felt he deserved more than being a mere butler. But things would never be any different, now that Elizabeth lay claim to a share of his lover. George watched as Lord Charles consumed many glasses of champagne having cheers with all his gentry friends; he could see his mind was becoming clouded. Was he trying to fob off Elizabeth so he could return to their bed tonight? Today had affected him more than he thought it would: Lord Charles looked so regal, he felt sad just being a bystander ... in fact, just a servant really!

All the guests had departed, but for Mr and Mrs Barnaby who hung back to wish the newlyweds a happy and prosperous marriage. Mr Barnaby kissed his daughter and whispered in her ear, "Be kind to Lord Charles tonight, make him happy." "I will, father, I promise," answered his dutiful daughter. Father and daughter were close, as they both wanted the best from life, and now she had the very best. A firm handshake was shared between the two men; one elated with this union, for the other it was a union of convenience. Elizabeth took Lord Charles by the hand and led him inside. He asked her to come to the drawing room, and there, in all its glory, stood a beautiful new piano. "This is your wedding present from me. Please play for me?" he asked. She sat down and began to play, then burst into song. Her voice echoed down the hallway until it reached George, who was sulking in bed. He sat up. Was this Elizabeth's voice? It sounded beautiful. He crept along the hallway to the drawing room and watched as Lord Charles sat gazing at his bride. Had she captivated him? Where did this leave him? He felt sad and let down at this moment, so he crept back to his room, climbed under the bedclothes and sobbed his heart out.

Lord Charles didn't want the singing to finish, but he was taken out of this moment by Elizabeth's hand, as she took his and led him through to her bedroom. She remembered her father's last words to her, 'tonight, make him happy'. She discarded her dress and was left standing in her beautiful silk undergarments, waiting for them to be removed by her husband. But he took his leave and went to the bathroom, where he nervously removed his clothes, wondering if he was going to be able to fulfil his obligations to Elizabeth tonight. Nothing was happening to his body so he wrapped a towel around his waist and came back to the bedroom. Elizabeth was still standing in her underclothes. What is wrong with her, why isn't she in bed? he wondered. "What is wrong?" he asked. "I am waiting on you to undress me, and look at my body." "Please, get into bed, Elizabeth," he politely told her. Poor Elizabeth, she was so taken aback she did as was asked of her, but what about her beautiful matrimonial nightdress, did he not want to see her in it? She had taken hours to carefully select the most alluring one in the store, one that would make any man's heart race. Everyone else's but not Lord Charles's!

She undressed and climbed into bed. "Now that we are married you may call me Charles, but on official duties I expect to be called by my peerage," he told her. He lay on his back and Elizabeth noticed his eyes slowly closing, so she moved close to him and took charge of his manly parts. But there was nothing happening down there, what was wrong? she wondered. She snuggled up to him and started nibbling on his ear. She felt him change his body position, he turned towards her, at last some action; was he ready to make passionate love to her? Charles remembered what was expected of him tonight, so he took her in his arms hoping for a miracle, which did eventually occur, so he performed his marital duty without an ounce of passion, rolled over and went to sleep. This was not what Elizabeth had imagined her wedding night to be. What happened to her dreams of romance, the touching, the getting to know each other's body parts, the pleasures she had felt in other men's arms while making love? They had not materialised with Charles. There he lay snoring in an ungodly fashion; she was thankful he had his own wing to go to at nights when he wasn't pleasing her. This was like the first time they had slept together at her home; he did his duty and there it ended, much like tonight. Was this going to be the sum total of her love life? Perhaps it would be a work in progress, she hoped so!

The next morning when Elizabeth woke, Charles was still asleep so she decided to make another move, to see if there were some pleasures yet to come. She slid her hand under the cover and worked her way to his manly parts; yes, something was happening there. This woke Charles; he expected to see George lying beside him, and when he realised it was Elizabeth, he scrambled out of bed and hurried to the bathroom, got himself dressed, and said to her as he was passing, "I'll see you at breakfast shortly," and left. Elizabeth couldn't control her tears. Not once had he passed a nice compliment to her or made her feel of any value at all; had she just become a household chattel, like her mother? No wonder she turned to the bottle for comfort! No, this is not going to be my life, she told herself.

She bathed, then dressed and went to the dining room, where she was met by George and Charles. They had already started their breakfast, but what was the butler doing eating at their table? She would speak to Charles about this later. It just meant they couldn't hold private conversations while he was present. She wanted to ask Charles if she had made him happy last night, but now she would have to wait. "What would you like for breakfast, Lady Elizabeth?" asked the cook. Lady Elizabeth, this sounded so upper class, she could begin to enjoy this title. "Just tea and toast will be fine, thank you," she answered. "What are we going to do today, Charles? Can we go riding?" Elizabeth asked. "Later in the day. I have business to attend to this morning," he told her. "Would you like me to help you with anything today, Lady Elizabeth?" asked George. "Yes, the piano has to move forward a bit, as I need a little more light behind me when I am playing." With this the men took their leave, thus leaving Elizabeth to dine on her own. She was going to take a carriage to pick up the rest of her wardrobe, then she could really settle into her new surroundings. This was her new home, and it was indeed a grand estate. Once she got her love life on track, then all would be what she had wished for. Then perhaps a son for Charles!

Elizabeth had insisted that she and Charles dined on

their own for breakfast, without George at the table. This Charles gave in to, but he was to be present for lunch and supper, as this had always been so, long before Elizabeth came on the scene. Begrudgingly she agreed to Charles's wish. Some of his decision-making she found strange, like not being allowed into his private wing. They shared everything ... or did they? Being the lord of the estate did entitle him to privileges that she couldn't question, but it did leave her wondering why this was out of bounds to her. She knew George had a room in that wing, perhaps that was why. Sadly, she had not made any progress with Charles and his bedroom manners. Sometimes weeks would go by and he never came to her room, then when he did turn up it was all very businesslike; no attention was given to what she wanted. It was as if he was there to do the deed at hand as quickly as possible, then take his leave. He slept over on the odd night, but this was only after he had been drinking. He would fall asleep sometimes before finishing the deed at hand, and he would just roll off and start snoring. Elizabeth felt used and abused when this happened, it just showed her how interested he was. She was sure the only reason they slept together was so he could get his son.

The wheat crops had been kind to the gentry this season, the prices were higher, there were no problems to import their wheat into England, and only a slight rise in shipping fees. The farms that had been sold only made a slight difference. The Irish economy was picking up a little, they were growing enough of their own wheat, so they didn't have to import it back to Ireland, thus holding the wheat prices to an affordable level. This was good news to Irish households, for they had struggled long enough. But did the estate owners share their profits with their tenant farmers? No. Did they reduce the land tariffs? No. The poor Irish tenant farmer was barely making a living, while the gentry lived in luxury. This was where the divide was, the poor versus the wealthy. But no-one in England cared that their king took the lands from their rightful owners, the Irish people; this was best forgotten.

Now it was time to call a board meeting and invite the solicitor whose client had bought the farms. They were ready to buy them back from the mystery buyer. The meeting was arranged for Thursday at two o'clock. This was Elizabeth's first board meeting, and she was expected to entertain the gentry in the drawing room alongside George. Charles thought a tune on the piano would go down well in the background while the men were consuming their drinks and hors d'oeuvres. Mr Barnaby would indeed be pleased to see his daughter had settled in at the Rothchild estate. All Charles had to do was to contact the solicitor and make sure he could attend; he would do this today.

Mary's solicitor was surprised to be asked to attend the meeting, but he had a fair idea what it would be about. He wouldn't even bother to contact Mary, as now that she had secured the farms, she would never give them up. It just meant she could look after more of her fellow countrymen. There was nothing in the sale agreement to say the farms had to be given back. The only clause was: 'if the buyer wanted to sell them, then they had to be offered back to the original owners first'. The landowners had signed the agreement under these terms so there was no comeback on the buyer. He had kept Mary up to date on what was happening at the estate as promised. She was not surprised to hear that Charles had married a neighbour's daughter, as she would be of his standing.

He certainly wouldn't settle for anything less, not Lord Charles!

The gentry were arriving at the Rothchild estate for their first board meeting of the new season. The atmosphere was certainly more jubilant than this time last year, as now they had money to spend. This season's yield had been kind to them and prices had stayed high. Last year had been a disaster, they had experienced what it was like to have the world against them; perhaps this was a little taste of what it was like to suffer. Payback perhaps! But today that was all forgotten, they were here to buy back their farms, their purses were flush. The last person to arrive was the solicitor, but this had allowed the business part of the meeting to be finished. He was welcomed and asked to sit up front, as there would be questions asked of him. "We have invited you here today because we have had a good season and the men would like to buy their farms back," stated Lord Charles. All eyes were fixed upon this one man! "Yes, we would like to start proceedings as soon as possible," said one of the affected owners. "I'm sorry, gentlemen, what do you expect me to do? The silent owner does not want to sell them," said the solicitor. "But the understanding was, we could buy them back." "That was when and if she wanted to sell them, but she does not want to sell," replied the solicitor. As soon as the word 'she' was mentioned, bells started ringing. Could that bloody Irishwoman Mary have bought them? Surely not, they would never get them back. Lord Charles turned white with rage. "Was it my mother who bought the farms?" "I am not at liberty to disclose the buyer, they want to remain anonymous." "But we need them, this was just a temporary sale," someone stated. "That was not on the sale agreement you signed. What was stated was they would be offered back to you before they were offered to anyone else if they should come up for sale." The solicitor put them straight. The men were devastated, they needed their land back to keep their estates afloat. "Is there any way we can persuade the buyer to sell them back to us?" they asked. "I'm sorry, gentlemen, there is nothing more I can do. They are not for sale, that has been made quite clear to me. I am only acting on the buyer's behalf." "What if we put in a high offer, would they change their minds?" they asked. "I'm sorry, they are non-negotiable; no amount of money will buy them back. I was told just last week they will remain in Irish hands, as they are the rightful owners, it was originally their land." With this last statement Lord Charles knew then who had bought the land. This was his worst nightmare ... it was his mother! Even though she was gone from the estate she still haunted him, it was the Irish curse. Would it never leave? Thank goodness there were no other reminders; this was the end, as his hatred for the Irish had not changed.

Once the solicitor left the meeting, the mood had gone from one of hope to one of despair. Everyone had the same thoughts: they had been beaten by Mary yet again. What a bitch she had become. Why did Lord Albert fall in love with her? But in their hearts they all agreed she was an outstanding beauty, and any one of them could have loved her. In fact, they all wished she was their lover, God knows many had tried! But this was kept in each of their minds, not to be said out loud. These three farms were never going to be retrieved, they were lost to Ireland forever! Mary was now their nemesis; she was a very wealthy woman and the Irish loved her. The meeting was called to a close, nothing had been solved other than establishing who the new owner was.

They all went to the drawing room where they were greeted by Elizabeth and George. There was much discussion about the lost farms, and three very sad estate owners would do battle to stay on their estates. If they were to remain they would have to cut their cloth to suit their now depleted incomes. Lord Charles asked Elizabeth to play the piano to take their minds away from the doom and gloom that had befallen the room. This along with a few whiskies lifted the tempo to one of pleasantness. When all the men left, Lord Charles went to his wing and sat at his desk venting all his hatred and anger towards his mother. He felt she was out to discredit him in front of the elite, but all Mary had done was seized on an opportunity, thanks to her solicitor who knew what was going on among the estate owners.

Several months had passed and Elizabeth was faced with morning sickness. She hadn't told anyone yet, not even Charles, as she wanted to be sure that everything was okay with her pregnancy. He hadn't been to her room lately, not that she minded, as his bedroom skills were still primitive; none of the fond memories of past lovers had taken place at the estate. Charles was certainly different ... somehow! Soon she would have a baby to love and care for, and this would compensate for the lack of love from Charles. She felt the title of 'Ladyship' didn't come without complications, but she was free to live a privileged life, even if she had to dream of past loves. Mr and Mrs Barnaby would be thrilled with the news; their grandson, if indeed it was a son, would one day be the lord and heir to the Rothchild estate.

Elizabeth would hold on to her secret for a little longer; these cherished thoughts were hers alone. Charles hadn't made any references to children, but just in passing conversation one day, he did mention he wanted a son and heir. That night she had a visit from Charles, much to her surprise, not to her delight. He had been drinking and fumbled his way into her bed. She was a little frightened as he seemed agitated and behaved roughly with her. She was annoyed and asked him to leave, but this met with a refusal. He tried to bed her, but his drunkenness took over and he rolled out of bed onto the floor. This is where she left him, out in the cold. She would have to tell him she was with child, as she feared for the unborn child. He would have to stop coming to her room. Little did she know the situation between Charles and George and that alcohol was used to block out what went on in his wing. When he woke in the morning and found himself lying on the bedroom floor, naked and shivering, he looked for Elizabeth but she was not there. He couldn't find his clothes so took a towel from the bathroom and wrapped it around him and made his way back to his wing. It was then he remembered what had happened last night: he had argued with George so took his revenge out on Elizabeth. He would find her and apologise for his cowardly behaviour, but she was nowhere to be found. The cook had seen her leaving in her carriage earlier.

Elizabeth had an appointment with her doctor to confirm her pregnancy. She was shaken today after last night's visit from Charles; his behaviour was unacceptable. If all was confirmed today, then he would not be welcome in her room until after the baby was born. She was told she was four months with child; this was truly a blessing in disguise. Now she could share her secret with everyone. She decided to stop off at her parents' estate and tell them they were going to be grandparents. This would create excitement, as this news was long waited for, unbeknown to Elizabeth. She met her father by the stables as she was tethering her horses. "Father, I have some good news. I am with child." "Elizabeth, that is wonderful, I'm so happy, come and share this with your mother," and he put his arms around her as they walked towards the home. He called for his wife and she came to the door. "Elizabeth, tell your mother what you have just told me," he said proudly. "Mother, I am four months with child." "That is lovely, my own little grandchild, I'm so happy," and she took her in her arms. She hoped her daughter was happy with Lord Charles, as she had never taken to him. This was never talked about; it was a burden each had to carry on her own. They talked together for a short while, then it was time for Elizabeth to leave.

She was not looking forward to seeing Charles; she still felt hurt with his behaviour last night. As she was tethering her horses she heard her name being called: "Elizabeth, where have you been? I've been looking everywhere for you." She looked around to see Charles walking towards her. "I want to apologise for last night," he said. "Charles, you hurt me. I am four months with child, I don't want you to visit me until after our baby is born." "Why didn't you tell me about the baby? I had a right to know!" he shouted. "I wanted to be sure. I have just come from the doctor, and he has just confirmed this to be true." Charles calmed down and reached for his wife's hand. "I'm happy for us both, come and sing to me?" he asked. They walked hand in hand to the drawing room where Elizabeth sat down at the piano. She played and sang, this seemed to bring calm and secureness to Charles. George heard Elizabeth's voice so came to listen to her; she sang beautifully. Charles beckoned for him to come and sit with him, then he told him the news about the baby. Waves of happiness and sadness both ran through George's mind. Now he would have to share him with three instead of two. Was he being pushed further away? But he had to admit, Lord Charles spent very little time in Elizabeth's bedroom.

4

The Return of the Irish Curse

There was only one week to go before the baby's due date. On Elizabeth's request, Charles had not been back to her room, but he didn't mind, as he preferred George's company. They had discussed male names for the baby and Charles decided he would be named Albert, after his father. In the future, after Charles's time, there would be Lord Albert II in charge of the estate. A girl's name was left to Elizabeth to choose, as the talk always centred around a son and heir. She spent most of her time at the piano, it was rest, and she was happiest when she sang. They had set up a nursery for the baby, next to Elizabeth's room, tradition being it was the mother's responsibility to care for and bring up the children. The father did very little in the rearing of children; this was aristocracy and the gentlemen were just that ... gentlemen, especially a lord!

The due day came and went but nothing was happening and Elizabeth was starting to panic. She hoped nothing was wrong with the baby, but her doctor had assured her the first child could come late, not to worry!

Now two weeks overdue, the doctor requested that Elizabeth come to the hospital. That night she went into labour and after a painful eight hours she gave birth to a little boy. The baby was taken away from her before she saw him, as she needed sleep. Lord Charles was informed of the birth of his son, so quickly drove the carriage to the hospital. The first person he asked to see was his son, before enquiring about his wife. This was noticed by the nurse. When the baby was passed to him, he took one look and handed it back to the nurse, challenging that it was not his baby. This little creature had red hair, where did this come from? The nurse knew Mary when she lived at the estate, so reminded Lord Charles of his Irish heritage. This he didn't want to know about, he had got rid of all Irish traits when his family left the estate. Now this; no way could a red-haired son rule an English estate. This child was now an outcast, he was doomed right from birth. The Irish curse had reared its ugly head again. Then he remembered his mother's words: "Don't forget you have Irish blood flowing through your veins." Was this all due to her?

He was furious and he felt nothing for this child. This was not what he wanted, why couldn't Elizabeth produce an English son? He would not be called Albert, that would be an insult; he was not deserving of this name. He would rename him John. The nurse saw this all unfolding and tears crept into her eyes. This was almost the case of the wrong baby scenario! Lord Charles saw the other babies and none of them had red hair. "Could we swap him and give him to someone else?" he asked the nurse. She was horrified; in all her nursing career she had never been asked to do this. "He is your son, your flesh and blood, yours and Elizabeth's." With this he left the room. He couldn't face Elizabeth; fancy her producing a baby with red hair! He felt sick, he needed to be comforted by George, so he drove back to the estate. He ran to their wing to find George making the bed. "Come here, George," and he cried in his arms. "What is wrong, Lord Charles?" he asked. "Elizabeth has produced a child with red hair, he can never be lord of the Rothchild estate." "But why? Your family all had red hair, they were of Irish blood like yourself," replied George, wondering what all the drama was about. "Don't ever mention that in this home. I am not Irish, I am English, I am my father's son, not my mother's. I hate the Irish. This baby will never become lord of the Rothchild estate," he said with such hatred in his voice. George was shocked!

Elizabeth was just waking up after having given birth. She had slept for several hours, as it had been a hard labour. She asked to see her baby so the nurse brought him in and put him in her arms. It was love at first sight; she kissed him and told him she loved him. This again brought tears to the nurse's eyes, but not for the same reason as before; these were tears of joy. Thank God Elizabeth loved her little son. Such a different outcome to the outburst of her husband, fancy asking to swap his own flesh and blood, that was so unethical, all because of the red hair. What chance was this child going to have, if not for the love of his mother? Elizabeth asked if Lord Charles had been to see his baby. What could the nurse say? She was still distraught over his shocking behaviour. "He came, but you were asleep so he said he would come back later." "He will love our little son," said a proud Elizabeth. The nurse had to turn her back to once again hide her tears ... if only that was so.

Elizabeth couldn't wait for Charles to see their little Albert. She waited eagerly for him to arrive, but he did not come until near closing time. As he walked in she expected him to kiss her for giving him a son, but he just stood and looked at her. "Have you seen our little Albert?" she asked. "Yes, but his name will not be Albert, he will be named John." "But we had already decided to call him after your father," said a dismayed Elizabeth. "I will never call a red-haired child after my father. I am so disappointed, why couldn't he be born with English blood?" Poor Elizabeth, the tears flowed down her face, she did not expect this. He was just a little baby, what did it matter the colour of his hair? "Would you like to hold your son?" she asked. "No, thank you. Are you well?" he asked. "Charles, he is just a baby, our baby, please love him," she begged. "I'm sorry, Elizabeth, I hate red hair. Next time I want an English son," and with this he bent down and kissed her forehead, then said goodnight and left. The nurse saw Lord Charles leaving, so she went to see Elizabeth and found her sobbing into her pillow. She sat down on the bed and took her hand. Elizabeth told her what had unfolded, unaware that she had witnessed Lord Charles's petulant behaviour earlier. "He will come around, it might take time. This has happened before but it all ended well," she told Elizabeth. But this was far from the truth. It had never happened before, but she had to give her hope, God knows she would need it. "Thank you. I know Charles will think differently when the baby comes home," said a grateful Elizabeth through her tears.

The next day her parents came to visit. Her mother

asked to see the baby as she wanted to cuddle him, so the nurse brought him in. They were shocked to see the red hair, but quickly put this aside for the moment. Mrs Barnaby picked him up and cuddled him, and a bond had formed at that moment; this Elizabeth was grateful for. "Well done, Elizabeth, now Lord Charles has his heir," said her father. She left this for the moment, hoping Charles would think things over and change his mind. Her parents stayed for a little while and fussed over the baby. Mr Barnaby more so, as now his grandson would one day become Lord Rothchild. As they were leaving, they saw George the butler arriving with flowers. Were they for Elizabeth? George was so upset with Lord Charles's behaviour over his own son, he wanted to let Elizabeth know he was happy for her. He walked into her ward and there she was cuddling a little bundle. "Hi, Elizabeth, these are for you. How is the wee man?" he asked. "Oh, thank you, George, they are lovely. Yes, baby is fine." "Can I hold him?" he asked. This took her by surprise, "Yes, he will love that," and she passed the baby to him. As George nursed him, he made baby noises, making them both laugh. "What a dear wee soul," he told Elizabeth. This was the first bit of happiness she had had since giving birth. "George, is Charles coming to visit me?" she asked. The answer to this was no, but he couldn't tell her, so instead said, "I think he has a meeting to attend." "Oh well, I will be home in a couple of days." After George left, she held her baby in her arms and looked at him. She knew regardless of what Charles thought, she would give him enough love for the two of them.

Two days later Charles arrived with the carriage to bring mother and baby home. The nurse gave the baby to him to hold, just to see if things had changed, but no, he handed him straight back to Elizabeth. There was no show of affection or even recognition in his eyes for this little boy. She wondered what lay ahead for him, but she knew the mother's love would grow along with the baby. When they arrived at the estate, George was there to meet them. He was the ray of sunshine Elizabeth needed. "How is the little one today?" he asked. "He is lovely, look at him, George." With this he came over and lifted him from Elizabeth's arms. "Welcome home, little one," he said as they walked into the lobby. Charles was silent, as he was still upset that he had fathered a child with the Irish curse. He would never feel anything for him, all he brought were bitter memories of the Irish clan he thought he was rid of. Now he was faced with this reminder forever! No, he was never going to be named Albert; John it was. Elizabeth took the baby from George and went to her room to feed him. She loved her baby, he felt part of her, they would make it together. She settled him down in the nursery and kissed him lovingly before she closed the door. Now to face Charles; she needed some answers.

"Why has our baby's name changed Charles? He was to be called Albert," she demanded. "I told you I will not give father's name to a baby with Irish blood running through his veins." "But you are half Irish as well as English. Your father loved your Irish mother," said Elizabeth. "I am English, do not refer to me as Irish ever again. The baby will be called John." That was where the conversation finished. "I'm off to bed, goodnight," and off he stalked. Elizabeth felt empty. She had never seen this side of Charles, but then there was his erratic behaviour in the bedroom at times. Was there something she didn't know?

As the days went by, Charles showed no interest in baby John, it was as if he was invisible. Elizabeth was thankful that George took an interest in him. He would often be seen holding him and lying on the floor beside him, trying to steal a smile. On sunny days Elizabeth would put him in his pram and walk around the estate, and sometimes George accompanied her. One day she asked him, "Why don't you find someone, George? You would make a good father, you are kind to baby John." If he could speak his mind, he would tell her that her son was the closest he would get to being part of any family, but of course, his dark secret would remain as such. "Perhaps one day," he answered, with a heart riddled with guilt. He had to admit he felt love for baby John, but was this because he was part of Lord Charles? He was finding Lord Charles's behaviour towards his son appalling, an innocent child being punished because of the colour of his hair. How could he not show him some love? He couldn't even talk to him about his son, it was dismissed instantly. What of his future?

It was baby John's first birthday tomorrow and Mr and Mrs Barnaby were coming to tea. Elizabeth begged Charles to be there and celebrate this special day as a family. She had everything organised, only one day to go! That night as she lay in bed she heard the bedroom door open and there stood Charles. He came to her bed, undressed and climbed in beside her. This was his first visit since the baby's birth. She had not missed him, especially after his last visit, which was still fresh in her mind. "I want an English son this time, Elizabeth," he whispered in her ear, as he took control and bedded her. When he left, she sobbed her heart out. Did he not remember who had the Irish blood and whose genes the red hair came from? Being Lady Rothchild was a far cry from what Elizabeth had imagined her life to be. Where were all the dreams that came with such a title? She was envied by many young ladies, but that envy only led to disappointment and despair and a life lived behind a charade.

Today was John's birthday. He was a happy baby and brought much joy to Elizabeth and even George, but not to Charles. He had never sat him on his knee, nor bestowed a single kiss upon his little head. This hurt both Elizabeth and George, but neither could change what was a gross injustice to this innocent being. George gave him a lovely teddy bear for his birthday, which brought tears from Elizabeth, as Charles had given him nothing, not even a birthday kiss. Her parents arrived with lots of little gifts for the birthday boy. They had accepted the Irish hair; after all, this was their daughter's child, one who would be lord one day! Elizabeth never mentioned to her parents what went on at the estate; this was her burden to bear, as no-one talked outside their marriage. The only person who saw the sadness Elizabeth endured was George. His feelings for Lord Charles were not as strong as they used to be; he saw deep hatred in his eyes that blurred his vision, thus leaving him devoid of feelings for those close to him, especially his son.

Although he attended his son's birthday, it was as if he weren't there, his thoughts were elsewhere. George was the one having fun coaxing John to crawl to reach his presents. They all laughed at the baby's antics, all except Charles. John was a happy soul who brought much joy to his mother. Later Elizabeth excused herself and took the baby to her bedroom to be fed, then she put him down for the night. Once the baby was out of sight, Charles's mood changed and he became more social, taking the top off another bottle of whisky. Elizabeth hoped this didn't mean another visit from Charles tonight. After her parents left she tidied up and then said goodnight, as she was tired. "No, you must play and sing to George and me," said Charles. "I'm sorry, Charles, I am tired, I'm going to bed." "You will sing before you leave this room!" he roared. "Come, Lord Charles, Elizabeth has had a big day, she has a baby to attend to," intervened George. "That baby will not come before me, now play the piano." She could see this was going to cause an argument, so she went to the piano and played with a heavy heart. After a short time, she announced, "I'm going to bed now," and left the room. Just as she was ready to drop off to sleep, she heard the door open; her worst fear was about to happen. It came with another warning: "Give me an English son this time."

Elizabeth had been to the doctor today and he confirmed she was with child. She had known this for several months but did nothing about it until now. This would leave her free of Charles; she would tell him tomorrow at breakfast. Today she took John for a walk in the forest just to get away from Charles. She was brokenhearted seeing the non-recognition of his own son. What was going to happen if she had another red-haired son? John was now four years old, so he would be off to school when the baby arrived. It had taken a long time for Elizabeth to be with child again, now everyone would be happy, the questions would stop, she would have peace! In the last few years nothing had changed with Charles; his son was still invisible to him. But to George, John was loved. How different could two men be? John had even called him 'Daddy' a couple of times when they were together. There had been many arguments over John's schooling. Charles wanted him sent off to a private boarding school at the age of five, but of course Elizabeth would not hear of this. She loved her son and she wanted him to go to the local school. George had been privy to these arguments and he was upset that Lord Charles could even think to send a five-year-old away.

This morning at breakfast Elizabeth told Charles she was with child. "Remember your promise to me, of an English son," he told her. "What do you mean, Charles? You have demanded this of me, but I can't promise you another son, this might be a daughter." "I want an English son," he demanded. "But you already have a son, an heir to the estate." "John will never be heir to the Rothchild estate," he hit back. "But I thought the first-born son became lord?" questioned Elizabeth. "I will have this law changed by royal pardon, in favour of my second son." Elizabeth could not believe what she was hearing. This meant John would have no standing in the Rothchild peerage line. If her next child was a girl, then this would put John back in line, so she hoped secretly that her wish be granted. Charles fought relentlessly to have John sent to boarding school so he wouldn't be reminded of the Irish curse; out of sight, out of mind. George sided with Elizabeth. How could anyone send a child away from a loving mother at the age of five? Elizabeth cried every day over this, but she would fight to the end. She knew she had George on her side.

As her pregnancy progressed, Elizabeth's health became an issue. She was distressed, as Charles's blatant disregard for John played on her mind. One day she and George took John into the woods to see the squirrels. They sat on a log and had a heart-to-heart talk. She said to George, "I want you to promise me, if anything happens to me, you will make sure John is okay. If Charles casts him out, please take him to his grandmother Mary in Ireland. She will love him for his Irish genes, as they came down from her." "Come, Elizabeth, nothing is going to happen," George assured her. "Please keep this promise to me, George, I beg of you." "Your promise will be kept," he told her from the bottom of his heart.

One night Elizabeth was woken with terrible pain and she knew something was wrong. She called for Charles, but he could not hear her. She dragged herself out of bed and along the hallway to Charles's wing. The pain was unbearable, she had to get to him. When she reached his room she opened the door and burst into his room. She got the shock of her life: there was Charles in bed with George. She felt sick, disgust overcame her, she panicked and tried to get away but the pain was too much and she fell to the floor, then everything turned to darkness. Charles jumped out of bed and pulled on his trousers then ran to Elizabeth, but she was unconscious. "Get the carriage, George, she has to get to the hospital," he yelled. George was in shock, he ran naked to the stables to hitch the carriage to the horses then brought them to the entrance. He helped Charles lift Elizabeth into the carriage. "Come, George, get some clothes on and drive us to the hospital." "What about John? We can't leave him here on his own," said a concerned George. "He's asleep, just leave him!" shouted Charles. "No, he must come with us, I will get him." With this he threw on some clothes and went to fetch John. By the time he got to the front entrance, Charles had gone. This meant Elizabeth was on her own in the carriage, while Charles was up front steering the horses. "What are we doing, George?" asked a sleepy John. George took him back to bed and tucked him in. He went straight back to sleep.

Poor Elizabeth, she had uncovered their deep secret. What a shock. He felt like a traitor; she had confided in him and he had let her down. What would happen when she came back home? Would she want him on the estate? The answer would be definitely not. She would hate him, and with these thoughts he burst into tears.

On arrival at the hospital Charles jumped down and called for someone to help him get his wife inside, she needed help. A nurse came running out and helped him lift Elizabeth into a chair until a bed was wheeled to the door. They rushed her into a ward and called for a doctor immediately. The nurse knew what was happening, Elizabeth was miscarrying, but they needed a doctor in case of complications. Lord Charles was asked to go to the waiting room; they would let him know what was happening as soon as the doctor had assessed her. He felt numb. What had Elizabeth seen? Would she remember? Was that the reason she fell to the floor? Was he going to be exposed, was his dark secret about to be made public? It was all about him, but what about Elizabeth? She was the one suffering, but that didn't seem to matter! As for George, he would speak severely to him. He was there to obey his orders, and when he refused to leave John and drive them to the hospital, that was not what he expected from him. It didn't take long before the nurse came out to tell Lord Charles that Elizabeth had lost the baby and she was very ill, still unconscious. She told him to go home and came back in the morning. He would have to speak with her first thing to make sure she didn't tell anyone what she had seen.

In fact, Elizabeth had opened her eyes, but asked the nurse to say she was still unconscious as she did not want to speak to Charles, ever! She was still very ill. She had visions of what she had seen in Charles's bedroom and was disgusted. Were they lovers? But George, she trusted him! It was all too much for her to take in, and she drifted off to sleep.

Later that night when Charles arrived home, he found George wrapped up in a blanket with John on the settee. They were sound asleep. "Wake up, George!" he said angrily. George was startled and sat up, frightening John who started to cry. "I'm staying here with John. He couldn't find his mother, he was upset." "Put him back in his bed and come to our room!" he demanded. "I am staying with him, he needs someone." "I need someone too!" he yelled. Never before had he taken a stance against Lord Charles, but he had had enough. "You are a grown man, John is but a child, this is where I will spend tonight," he said adamantly. With this, John cuddled into him in fear of his father. Lord Charles stomped out like a spoilt child.

Something happened to George that night; his whole life changed in the blink of an eye. All his feelings for Lord Charles were gone; he saw him for who he really was. He would take his leave from the Rothchild estate when Elizabeth came home, then she could love and care for John. He was George's first concern, he actually loved the little boy. He would never have any children of his own, so John was special to him. But could he face Elizabeth? She would hate him, now that she knew he had deceived her. Tonight was going to be a long one for George, as he would try to work out where his future lay, but it certainly wasn't here with Lord Charles. He hoped Elizabeth would be home in a couple of days, as John would miss her. His father was of no help to him, he wouldn't even try in a crisis to give his son some stability, or a sense of belonging. He had dismissed him completely. 'How could I have feelings for someone so heartless?' George asked himself.

When George and John woke the next morning, Lord Charles had finished his breakfast and was at the stables. They sat and talked over breakfast, then John wanted to know if he could go to the hospital to see his mother. "You will have to ask your father," George told him. John walked over to the stables. "Father, can I visit mother?" but he was just ignored. He came back to George in tears. "He never talks to me, why?" he asked. "I don't know, John, but your mother and I love you. You are a good boy," and he ruffled his hair affectionately. George was so angry he walked over to the stables to talk to Lord Charles. "Can you not find it in your heart to speak to your son? He wants to see his mother. Have the decency to take him to the hospital, he is missing her." "The sooner he goes to boarding school, the better. Elizabeth will just have to get used to the idea. I don't want him here." George was so angry he slapped him across the face. "He is only a child, your child, how can you be so heartless?" he said, as he walked away totally disgusted, leaving Lord Charles standing there in shock. Fancy a servant striking his master; if he wasn't his lover, he would run him off his land. He hitched the carriage to the horses and drove off.

First stop was at the hospital; he had to see Elizabeth. When he arrived, the nurse took him to an office, as the doctor wanted to speak to him. "Elizabeth is very weak and we are worried. She is asking to see her son. Please go and bring him to her," he asked. "I will go and see her first," said Lord Charles. "No, she has requested to see John alone. Please do as she asks, it is very important that he comes straight away." Lord Charles was annoyed by this, but to save face he left to fetch John.

John was taken by the nurse to see his mother. She cried when she saw him, and asked him to sit beside her. "Are you sick, mother?" he asked. "Yes, John, but I want to tell you about your grandmother Mary in Ireland. She will love you, you have lots of cousins there. One day George is going to take you to meet her, but this is our secret. Don't tell your father, just talk to George about it, he knows." "But why can't you take me?" he asked. "I am very sick, but whatever happens, remember I love you dearly, so does George. Your lovely red hair comes from your Irish grandmother, you have Irish blood in your veins, be proud of this. I am tired now, lie here and cuddle me," and she kissed her son on the forehead and fell asleep. The nurse came in to see Elizabeth, and there on the bed she lay with her son in her arms. "Mother, wake up?" he was calling to her. The nurse knew then she was never going to open her eyes. "Come, John, let your mother sleep, she is tired." She took his hand and led him to his father. "Lord Charles, Elizabeth has gone to sleep, she has left us. Please take your son home and explain this to him." "But I didn't see her, why was he allowed to be with her?" he asked angrily. "Because he was the only one she wanted to see, she asked for him," stated the nurse. Charles knew deep down in his heart why she didn't want to see him, but now, thank God, his dark secret would never be exposed. Life would continue as normal with George, and John would be sent to boarding school. Then he would think of taking another wife to give him an English son.

He drove John back to the estate in silence. John knew his father never spoke to him, so he never asked him questions, as there would be no answers. George was the only one he could talk to. He remembered his mother's words about his grandmother Mary, so he would ask George, but not in front of his father. This had to be kept a secret between him and George. They pulled up at the stables and John ran to find George. "George, where are you?" he yelled. "I'm in the garden, John." He ran to find him. "How is your mother?" he asked. John told him she had gone to sleep with him in her arms, but he couldn't wake her. As soon as he heard this, he knew she had passed away. He clung to John and cried. "What's wrong, George?" "Did your father talk to you about your mother?" "Father never talks to me, you know that, George,. Why are you crying?" he asked. What could he say? How was he going to tell this little boy his mother would not be coming home, ever? "Come with me, John, we need to find your father." They walked into the home and found Lord Charles sitting in the drawing room. "Lord Charles, please tell John about his mother, he has to know." He looked at his son: "Your mother will not be coming home, she was very sick, she has died." Upon hearing these words about his mother, he clung to George and sobbed his little heart out. "But I love her, why has she left me?" he wanted to know. "Sometimes things happen, we don't want them to but we can't stop them. Your mother loved you dearly, she will always love you, please remember this," said a tearful George. "I will go and tell Mr and Mrs Barnaby about their daughter," and with this Lord Charles left.

"George, Mother told me you would take me to meet my grandmother Mary in Ireland one day. She said this was our secret, not to tell father. Did you know I am Irish?" he asked. "Yes, John, that is where your red hair comes from, she will love you. I made a promise to your mother and I will keep it." "Thank you, Daddy George," said the little boy as he clung to him.

The news was out about Elizabeth's death; no-one was more devastated than Mr Barnaby. Later on, there would probably be a new Lady Rothchild, but his grandson would one day be Lord Rothchild, nothing would change that, as he was the eldest son. Elizabeth did him proud. They were disappointed with John's Irish hair, but they put on a brave face for Elizabeth's sake. Mrs Barnaby worried about little John, whose mother loved him dearly, but whose father didn't have much to do with him. She had never liked Lord Charles, not that she could say that in front of her husband. All the men adored him! They did wonder about the butler, who seemed to have taken John under his wing. In fact, it was him who took flowers to Elizabeth in hospital. Was there something between them? Surely Elizabeth wasn't that foolish!

Condolences were arriving from everywhere and everyone, as Lord Charles was a well-known man. Clients from his law practice, as well as his gentry friends, would all be there tomorrow for the funeral to support him at this sad time. Things were estranged at the estate since Elizabeth's death. George had elected to move into John's wing, to be close to him at nights, as he was having bad dreams; he missed his mother. Lord Charles was irate with George over this decision, but once he sent John off to boarding school next week when he turned five, George would come back to their room and all would be back to normal; he missed him. At the moment all his spare time was spent arranging Elizabeth's funeral, but after tomorrow it would all be behind him. He would be a free man; he and George would be together again. His marriage to Elizabeth didn't yield what he wanted, all he was left with was the 'Irish curse', but he would take a new wife and get his English son, then he would apply to have the title of Lord granted to his next son. It all sounded so simple; he had it well under control, he was a man of means!

Today was Elizabeth's funeral. George made sure John was dressed in his Sunday best, and he brushed his Irish hair so it would stand out, as he knew how much his mother loved the colour of his hair. This she would approve of, as she loved his Irish reminders; it so irritated Lord Charles. But today belonged to Elizabeth. John cried most of the morning as George explained what was happening, that they were going to say their final goodbyes to his mother. He would never see her again. The whole community turned out, as did all the eligible young ladies, helped along by their fathers; they were all vying for the new title of Lady Rothchild. Little did any of them know what accompanied that title! John held George's hand all through the service, as he was his best friend. John's grandparents were there but they didn't cuddle him like George. He looked at his father and felt nothing. He doesn't even like me, thought John. People came up to him and shook his hand, some even cuddled him and they all had tears in their eyes. They must have loved mother too, he thought. He didn't see any tears in his father's eyes but they were there in George's, because they were running down his cheeks. Everyone came back to the estate, and there were people milling around everywhere. George had to help the other servants serve the guests, so John wondered off on his own into the woods. This was where he and his mother sat, on this very log. He remembered his mother's words while he was lying in her arms on her hospital bed: '... your grandmother Mary in Ireland ... will love you, ... you have Irish blood in your veins ...". One day he would meet her and he would tell her these words.

John's fifth birthday had arrived. He was a big boy now,

and would be starting school soon. He had heard his father and George arguing in the drawing room, about him going to school. Why would they yell at each other? he wondered. The cook had made him a cake and his Barnaby grandparents were coming to his party, along with George. He was excited because it was his birthday, and also sad, for his mother wouldn't be there with him, but he knew she still loved him. His grandparents brought presents, but his best present came from George: a brand-new schoolbag made of leather; it smelt nice. "Father must have forgotten my birthday, he didn't get me a present," he told George. This was the final straw; what man would not take the time to buy his son a birthday present?

George knew his time at the estate was running out. But what John didn't know was going to come as a big shock to him. Everyone sang to him and he blew out all his candles with such pride. He was ready for school now. "When am I going to school, father?" he asked. "Tomorrow you will pack your clothes, then George will take you to the station and accompany you to your new school. You will live at this school with other boys." "But father, I want to stay here with George and go to school," he sobbed. "I have enrolled you and paid for you, so that is where you are going," he told him sternly. George left the room, he couldn't hide his tears any longer. He was heartbroken for this little boy; this was almost cruelty. John looked at his father and caught his glance; his eyes were cold, there wasn't a hint of kindness in them. "I hate you!" he yelled and ran out of the room. "Lord Charles, don't you think he is too young to send to boarding school?" asked Elizabeth's mother. "I will be busy now that Elizabeth's gone, he will be better out of the way." This just confirmed what she had always thought of him, a pompous, self-opinionated man whom she never liked nor trusted. Of course, Mr Barnaby agreed with Lord Charles; this was a stamp of authority among the gentry. The womenfolk were merely chattels, their voice didn't count for much.

George heard John outside in the garden crying. He went and sat beside him. "I'm sorry, John, I tried. I asked your father to let you go to the area school, but he wouldn't listen to me." "Is that why you were yelling at each other in the drawing room?" he asked. "Yes, but he is your father." "I wish you were my father, George. You are kind and I love you," he sobbed. "I will tell you a big secret, but your father must not know. When you go to boarding school, I will leave here and get a job in the same town, then we can see each other often," he whispered in John's ear. "Would you do that for me? You are my best friend. That's why I love you, George," he said in all innocence. "John, your grandparents are leaving, come and say goodbye," called his father. He went to the front entrance where they stood. His grandfather shook his hand and said, "Good luck, John, do well at school." His grandmother cuddled him and told him to write to her, then she whispered, "Your mother will be proud of her big boy." This brought a smile. "Goodbye, grandmother."

The packing was done, all John's clothes were in suitcases and his favourite things were in his schoolbag, the one that George gave him. The gardener drove them to the station; they just had to wait for Lord Charles to come and say goodbye to his son. The train was nearly due, but where was his father? They waited and waited, then the train arrived so they had to board. He never even made it to see his son off to school. George and John chatted all the way on the train. He was happy in George's company. He didn't know where he was going, but George did. It was all new to them both. The train stopped at Wakefield station. This was their stop, so they gathered up their bags and cases and walked up the platform. They found a carriage that was picking up new students and taking them to the school. They climbed aboard the carriage. The driver knew where he was going, this was his job, to safely deliver the students. As they slowed down to go through the school gates, the buildings ahead looked very large and the gardens were huge. George saw a poster on the gates: 'Vacancy. Wanted, gardener, apply within'. Was this his opportunity? It would mean he could see John every day. He would speak to the person in charge as he registered John. He had experience as a gardener at a posh college, that was how he met Lord Charles. He left his details with the registrar and they would contact him in a week. Now it was time to say goodbye to John. They both cried as they hugged each other. "Remember our secret, John, it won't be long. Don't write to me, I will come and see you as soon as I move here. We don't want your father to know as he will be angry with me for leaving him." "But he can find another butler, George," answered John casually. If only it was that easy, thought George.

5

George Moves On

A week had gone by and still George had not moved back into their shared bed. Lord Charles was becoming angry. They were arguing a lot; he wanted George to move back in with him, he was lonely. George had asked for another week on his own, hoping he would hear back from John's school. The long-awaited letter arrived and he had been accepted for the position of gardener, and was asked to start in two weeks. How was he going to tell Charles? Would he confront him, or leave him a letter? Since Elizabeth discovered their dark secret, George's life had changed. He often wondered if this contributed to her premature death. Did he help take John's mother away from him? Is this why his feelings switched from Lord Charles to John? Did he owe it to him, for Elizabeth's sake, as he really had no-one else? Only a father who blamed everyone else for the Irish misgivings that had come through in his genes. Elizabeth had asked him to take John to meet his Irish grandmother; this was their secret, this promise he would not break.

He could not find it in his heart to stay in a relationship that had broken two hearts that believed in him. He felt he had betrayed Elizabeth. Lord Charles was not the man he wanted to be with any more. He had no feelings for his own flesh and blood. What would happen to him when Charles didn't want him any more, he would be an outcast. George felt it was his duty to care for John. He had lost the one that loved him most, he was only a child who was placed in a boarding school at the age of five, away from all he knew.

The day had arrived for George to take his leave. He waited until Lord Charles left for his office, then he packed his bags. He had taken several nights to put together a letter, explaining why he couldn't be with him. His feelings for him had gone, there was nothing left for him to give. He was leaving to start a new life, this would be the last contact he would have with him. Then he placed the letter on Lord Charles's pillow. He asked the gardener to drive him to the station. "Are you going on holiday, George?" he asked. "Yes, I'm taking a month off." "Well, have a good time, see you when you get back." George didn't answer. He took his suitcases from the carriage and walked along the platform to the awaiting train. His services as a butler were over, he was returning to the job he loved. He settled into his seat and watched as Surrey passed by. His thoughts went to John; he wondered how his life at boarding school was faring. It was one month since he had left and he missed him. He didn't know if he had written to his father, as nothing had been said at the estate. Tomorrow he would go to the school and make final arrangements for his new position and hopefully catch up with John.

Lord Charles had decided to leave his office earlier today as George had promised to move back into their room. He bought an expensive bottle of whisky to celebrate what seemed like a long parting. He had missed him, the estate had felt sterile lately, what with Elizabeth gone and no George to share his bed. No thoughts went to his own son, he never fitted into the equation. When he finished tethering the horses he walked towards the home with his bottle of whisky. "George, I'm back, where are you?" he called. The gardener heard Lord Charles calling, so came to see what he wanted. "No, I was calling for George," he said. "But he has gone on holiday, I took him to the station this morning." Lord Charles was shocked; no, this couldn't be right. He took off into the home and ran to his bedroom. There on the pillow was the letter. Had something happened that he had to leave? He tore it open and began reading: 'Lord Charles, these are my final words to you. We will never meet again. Since the day Elizabeth entered our room and found us in bed together, I can't help but think we both contributed to her death. For this I have suffered, as has your son, who lost the most precious person in his life. Your detachment from him has robbed me of any feelings for you; each day they grew less as he grew older. John is your own flesh and blood, your only reminder of Elizabeth, and you chose to ignore this child. You are the reason he was born with red hair, you are the one with Irish blood running through your veins. None of this was his choosing, but you are a coward to take this out on a child who is too young to defend himself. A lord, you may be, but your actions are those of a lesser man. One day you will suffer as John has done, only then will you learn that there is such a thing as forgiveness. You are no longer worthy of my love. Goodbye forever. George.' "No, this is not true, you are my only love, George, don't leave me!" he yelled in disbelief. "Please don't leave me," he sobbed, then his anger turned into uncontrollable rage. He threw the letter on the floor, ripped all the bedclothes off the bed and lay on the bare mattress pounding it with his fists. This was his worst nightmare, to be abandoned by his lover. George had been part of his life for nearly nine years, since his boarding school days. He was the handsome gardener and Charles was the head boy at the college. The more he thought of George, the harder he pounded. This continued until all his physical strength was gone; now it was time for the tears. He sobbed like a child, reaching for the pillow and he hung on to it, as if it were George in his arms. A dark cloud descended, then there was nothing, his body went limp, his mind gave out on him, he lay motionless on the bed.

When he woke he was shivering, there were no covers on the bed and he was lying on the bare mattress. Then it all came flooding back, reality struck, he was on his own, George was gone forever. He reached for the letter and read it again. This time the pain was less, as he knew what the letter contained, but he was bewildered why George blamed himself for Elizabeth's death. If she had obeyed the house rules, she should never have entered their bedroom, it was out of bounds, and for this she suffered the consequences. Never mind that she was in pain, rules were rules! As for John, he was no more than an 'Irish curse' given to him, to make him suffer, but in the end, it would be John that suffered; because of him, he had lost George.

Even in his darkest hour Lord Charles could find no blame with himself. He pulled some bedclothes from the floor to cover himself and went back to sleep. He wasn't ready to face the world without George.

Today George rode out to the boarding school. It was lunch time and all the boys were sitting in groups having lunch on the grass. He looked to see if he could see John among them, but he was not there. Then he spotted a lonely figure sitting on his own; it was John, his red hair the giveaway. George's heart sank. Was this poor boy still suffering? Even at school he could not escape sadness; when was his life going to amount to something? He made his way over to John, who jumped up and ran to him when he realised it was George. "I've missed you, George. I have waited every day for you to come," he said as he hugged him. "I've missed you too, John. I am now the gardener here, so we will see each other every day. Do you like it here?" George asked. "Not really, I haven't made any friends. The boys are all older than me. You are still my best friend," he told George. "Don't worry, John, we will change this when I start here next week. Have you written to your father?" "Yes, but he hasn't answered my letters. Only Grandmother Barnaby writes to me." He fondly ruffled John's hair. "You are a good boy. Don't tell your father that I work here, this is our secret." "We have two secrets now, this one and Grandmother Mary's," he said in all earnestness. "I have to go now, George, see you next week!" he yelled as he ran towards the classrooms. For a child who had faced so much rejection, he was handling himself remarkably well, thought George. But no-one knew that he was suffering silently in his heart.

6

Five Years On

~

Today Lord Charles was marrying Anne Cleave, the daughter of a wealthy estate owner who lived on the north side of Surrey. So, this was another match made in heaven, just like his first one; two prominent families brought together by marriage. The Barnabys would not be there as Mr Barnaby had passed away and his wife was hospitalised, as her drinking had worsened so she needed full-time care. Their sons now owned the estate. John had not been told of his father's wedding. He had stopped writing to him, as he never had answers to his letters over the past five years. The wedding was a flash affair; Lord Charles wanted all the pomp and ceremony he deserved. He was the wealthiest landowner in Oxshott, his law practice was thriving and the wheat yields had been kind to him, as with all the estate owners. The three farms that had to be sold off because of hardships had never come back to their owners. They remained in the hands of the

Irish owners. Over the years it had been established that Mary O'Leary, once Mary Rothchild, was the silent buyer of the land. This was to the disgust of the English gentry, especially to think it had reverted back to Irish ownership. But did they forget they were the rightful owners? This had fuelled even more hatred in Lord Charles towards his family. John had never been asked home for the school holidays, it was as if he was a ward of the state.

Things had changed at the estate since George left. Lord Charles had never recovered from losing him and try as he did, he couldn't find a replacement lover. So now it was down to the business of producing an English son to carry on the peerage and the estate; it had to stay in the Rothchild name as it had done for many generations. Thus his marriage to Anne. Anne was quite a headstrong young lady, not at all submissive like Elizabeth, this Lord Charles would soon find out. But today was one of celebration, she was to become Lady Rothchild, a name that she would use to her advantage. The name was more important to her than Lord Charles himself. Was this really going to be a match made in heaven, or more importantly, a name taken in marriage? Either way there would only be one winner. Anne was a beautiful bride, she was outgoing and popular, a pillar of society, one who would enhance Lord Charles's standing. They were both in this partnership for gain. All Anne had to do was to give her husband a son, an English one at that.

The vows had been taken, now they were Lord and Lady Rothchild. The title of Lord had been dropped by Charles in their private life. They mixed with everyone, Anne being the perfect hostess, flirting with the men; they all loved her. The drink was flowing freely and Charles was participating along with his friends. He needed some

Dutch courage for later, as he had not bedded Anne. In fact, nothing had happened in that department since George left, five years ago. His main duty now was to father the son he wanted. As the party drew to a close and everyone had gone home, there were only two people left, Charles and Anne. "Anne, I want to inform you, I have my own private wing and when I want to bed you I will come to your room. Your wing will be yours and the children we have. The nursery will be next to your room." "That's fine," said Anne. This suited her, as she didn't find Charles all that attractive, it was the name that was of most interest to her. This meant she had her own privacy, in her own wing, only to be distracted when Charles visited, which she hoped wasn't going to be too often. She would fulfil her duty to him and give him the son he desired. She hadn't met his other son yet, but she hoped to see him in the school holidays when he came home.

Anne went to her wing and prepared for bed. She had bought some glamorous nightwear for Charles's benefit; would he visit her on her wedding night? She lay in bed waiting, then she heard her bedroom door opening and in staggered Charles. He had gone to his room and consumed Dutch courage out of a whisky bottle, then undressed and staggered along the hallway totally naked to Anne's bedroom. When she saw him and the condition he was in, she told him to go straight back to his wing and come back tomorrow night when he was sober. Never had he been turned down before in his own home. His pride was hurt, which did nothing for his ego, or anything else for that matter, so he left the room. This behaviour Anne would not stand for, as he was less attractive when he had been drinking, therefore she would not share her bed with him. He would soon learn she had standards!

The next morning at breakfast Charles was very subdued. His eyes diverted away from Anne's when she looked at him. "I will not entertain you in my bedroom in a drunken state. It may have happened before, but not with me," she let him know. Poor Charles, he felt deflated, he needed extra courage to be able to perform his marital duties, as he was uncomfortable in women's company. He could not display his feelings; this went back many years, as was experienced by his mother and sister. He thought they were beneath him, that he was superior to them, hence his love affair with George. He needed the extra courage so he could be masterful while performing his duty. He excused himself and said he was leaving for his office, he would be home for supper. As he was about to leave Anne came over and kissed him goodbye. She was affectionate outwardly, but her bedside manner was yet to be determined. Would he find out tonight?

Now that Charles was away for the day, Anne decided to rearrange everything in the home to her liking; she had to be happy. The butler was called in to help move large objects. He was an older man and did as Lady Anne asked. There were items she didn't like, so they were moved to the outside sheds; tomorrow she would replace them with things that pleased her. Anne enjoyed being the lady of the estate; she was a young lady who knew where her life was going to take her. All she had to do was produce a son and then perhaps a daughter, then her duties with Charles would be over, and she could proceed to be a lady. She was so different to Elizabeth, who was dutiful and a little afraid of Charles. No-one frightened Anne! When Charles arrived home he didn't know himself. Where was everything? He was upset. "Anne, come here!" he roared. "What has happened to my home?" "No, it is our home, I am your wife, I have to be happy here too." Charles could not believe what he had just heard. No woman apart from his mother had talked to him like this. "You have to ask for my permission before you make changes. This is my estate, it has been in my family for generations," he said angrily. "Charles, you took me as your wife, I will give you children, therefore this becomes my home for life, so I will live among things I like." He could see she was a headstrong young lady. He hadn't noticed this before, he just presumed she would do what was expected of her, like Elizabeth had. Most wives of the landowners were submissive, but Anne was not. She was, in fact, the spoilt daughter of a wealthy estate owner, much like Charles. He went to his wing to mull over this conversation, never before had he met someone that would stand up for herself against him. She reminded him of his mother, Mary, who he wanted to forget. He felt cheated; fancy her with three new farms and of course her Irish blood, giving him a son with red hair. Had he made a wrong judgement marrying Anne? He began to doubt his decision, but alas was it all too late?

They sat down to supper together and Anne talked to Charles about their friends, and how she would plan parties on the estate. "We must have parties here, Charles, this will put us in the limelight." He had to admit that life was less complicated with George gone, as he had nothing to hide, other than his feelings, as not a day went by that he didn't think of him. He was his one love! But now it was an heir to the estate he needed to concentrate on, and once he was born, Charles would proceed with the law change that would allow the second son to become Lord. He would do this through a 'Royal Licence'. Being a lord hopefully would give him some leverage.

Tonight, Charles had plans to consummate his marriage; the sooner Anne became with child, the sooner he would get his son. He was nervous, almost frightened, but it was a deed that had to be done. He made his way to Anne's room, opened the door and walked in. "Charles, you must knock before entering a lady's room." This he did not expect, especially in his own home. "I have never knocked before," he said. "Then you don't know how to treat a lady. In future when you visit me, you will knock." Poor Charles, any courage he had mustered had suddenly disappeared. He felt flat and deflated, his ego had been crushed. "Come over and get into bed," she told him. He slowly undressed and slid between the sheets, unsure what would happen next. He lay there, then he felt Anne's hands searching his body. This made him feel uncomfortable; he was the master, and with this thought everything came to life. He forced himself on her with no regard to her wants, did what had to be done, rolled off, then climbed out of bed and went to his room. This left Anne feeling empty and disappointed. She hoped it wouldn't take many of these meetings before she was with child. Then she would be relieved of Charles's visits.

John was now ten years old. Over the past five years at boarding school, he was one of the longest boarders. George made sure he had friends, he taught him how to interact with the boys and become involved in sports. He had grown into a strong lad. He was like a son to George, the son he would never have. But George still lived with the guilt that he had a hand in Elizabeth's death, thus his dedication to John. John had not been back to the estate since he was sent to boarding school. There had been no correspondence from his father, but this didn't worry him too much, he had put up with this most of his young life. At least he had George! Then one day a letter arrived from an Anne Rothchild. John opened it to find his father had remarried and Anne was his new wife. She wanted to meet him, so asked him to come home for the school holidays. He was surprised, in fact shocked that his father wanted him to come home. But unbeknown to John, Anne had taken it upon herself to invite him, without Charles's knowledge. John showed the letter to George; they were both a little baffled, but George encouraged him to go. Perhaps this was the end of an estranged relationship. He told John he would accompany him to Oxshott, as he wanted to meet his grandmother Mary's solicitor, to get her address and find out where she lived in Ireland. He felt it was time to keep his promise to Elizabeth. The holidays were in a week's time.

John and George were on the train, on their way to Oxshott. George had to be careful as he didn't want to run into Lord Charles. He was only going to spend a night there, then would catch the train back to Wakefield tomorrow. John was nervous, it was five years since he had seen his father. When they stopped at the station and John alighted from the train, he saw a young lady standing on the platform, whom he presumed was Anne. She was a good-looking lady, so he called out to her. She looked at him and got the shock of her life. Where did that red hair come from? It looked like an Irish trait. She was not prepared for this. "Hello, are you John?" "Yes," he answered in a quiet voice. There were no photos of him on the estate, which she thought was strange, so she didn't know what to expect. "Come, I have the carriage behind the station, we will drive back to the estate." George had been slow getting off the train as he thought Lord Charles may have been there to meet John. He should have known better! He waved to John as he left the station.

On the way back to the estate, Anne chatted away to John, asking all about his life at boarding school. She was shocked to hear he had never been home in five years. Why? she asked herself. That seemed strange, but perhaps she had better not ask John. Anyhow, his father would be happy to see him. This was going to be a lovely surprise for Charles when he came home. They would have a celebratory supper tonight, then have a catch-up in the drawing room. As they entered the home John couldn't believe how the décor had changed. "Gosh, this looks different." "Do you like it?" Anne asked. "Yes, it feels much more lived in, more colourful." "That's good, your father was angry at first, but I told him now that I was his wife, I had to feel comfortable here, that is why I changed things," she told John. He couldn't believe what Anne had just told him, perhaps his father had met his match! He was nearly five when his mother died, but he could still remember little bits and pieces, but he never forgot her words, 'I will always love you'. "I'm going into the woods to see the squirrels," he told Anne. As he made his way there, his thoughts went back to his mother; this was where they had spent time together. It was his favourite place on all the estate. He sat on a log and watched the squirrels. The thought of meeting his father left him a little afraid, but he liked Anne.

Lord Charles tethered his horses and made his way to the front entrance where he was met by Anne. "Charles, I have a nice surprise for you. Come into the dining room." She led him in and when he saw John sitting at the table, he turned red with anger. "What is he doing here?" he bellowed. Anne looked at Charles. "What do you mean, he is your son, this was meant to be a surprise." John got up and ran past them to his room, tears streaming down his face. "I am ashamed of you, Charles, the poor boy, you have embarrassed him," said a disappointed Anne. "He is of Irish blood, he will never become lord of this estate, that is why you must give me an English son," he told her. "I am going to fetch John, you will sit and have supper with us," she scolded him as she walked out to find John. He was lying on his bed crying. Why did his father hate him so much? "Come, John, have supper with us, show your father how brave you are, I will deal with him later." With this she came over and took his hand and led him out to the dining room. They sat and ate supper, but not once did Charles speak or even look at his son. Anne kept up conversation between her and John. This was her first insight into something that troubled her deeply. His own son was sitting at the same table and he ignored him, how sad was that? How was he going to treat their children? After supper John excused himself and went to bed. He would leave tomorrow and go back to boarding school. Perhaps George would be on the same train? He liked Anne, she was kind to him, but his father, he still didn't want anything to do with him.

The next morning when John made his way to the breakfast room, Anne was there on her own; Charles had left for work. "I'm sorry, John, I didn't know your father felt like this. It is shameful, his own son. I thought I would give him a nice surprise, instead you have been hurt, what can I say?" "Thank you, Anne, but I will leave today. Can you take me to the station, please?" "But where will you go?" she asked. "I will just go back to boarding school." "But it is the holidays, you should be home with your family," Anne said with a heavy heart. "I have never been home in five years, father leaves me at school, he doesn't care about me, I wish it was him that died, not my mother." "Oh John, that is so sad. One day we will have children, you will have half brothers or sisters, you must be part of their lives. I will work on your father," she assured him. "Thank you, Anne, you are kind, but I must leave, please take me to the station?" She asked the gardener to get the carriage ready, then she drove John to the station. Just as they arrived the train was pulling in and there was George climbing aboard. "George, wait for me!" he yelled as he said goodbye to Anne. She hugged him and told him he was a lovely boy, before she let him go. He must know that man George, it was nice to think he wasn't travelling on his own, she thought. She was so angry with Charles and his petulant behaviour, this would not go without an explanation.

George was surprised to hear John's voice. "Why are you coming back?" John told him the whole story, as the tears ran down his face. "Anne is a nice lady, she was angry with father, she said she will deal with him. I hope she does." "I'm so sorry, John. But I have good news: in the big holidays you and I are going to Ireland to meet your grandmother Mary. I will write to her and tell her about you and your mother's last wish, before she passed away." "Oh George, that would be wonderful, then I will meet her, I can't wait," said an excited young boy. Some deserved happiness at last, thought George. He thought back to his talk with Mary's solicitor and was shocked to learn the truths about Lord Charles. He knew nothing of the goings on at the Rothchild estate before he arrived there. The solicitor spoke very highly of Mary. George could remember seeing her the morning she left. She was a beautiful-looking lady, with the fiery red Irish hair. She would love her Irish-looking grandson, and George was sure he would love her in return. How Lord Charles could ever think of John as an 'Irish curse' left him cold. That was when all his feelings for him disappeared, that was the moment the relationship ended.

When Charles came home that night, he came in late, hoping to avoid sitting at the table with his son. "You're late," Anne greeted him. "Sit down, I want to tell you how petulant your behaviour was towards your son. He is a nice young lad and still you ignore him. He must hate you, as I would. Is this how you are going to treat our children? If so, there will be no babies. Grow up, Charles. At least John had a friend, George, who travelled on the train with him." "What do you mean, where was George?" asked Charles. "He was at the station, John seemed pleased to see him." Charles's heart missed a beat. George here in Oxshott, why didn't he know? Why didn't he contact him? God knows he had missed him. Just the mention of his name sent ripples down his body. He was the only person Charles felt comfortable with. He left the room, he needed time on his own to weep and dwell on those far-off memories. Would he ever come back? How did John know George was at the station? Were they in touch with each other? So many thoughts, they were messing with his brain. "George, why did you leave me?" he cried out in despair. But, he had explained to Charles in his letter why their relationship ended. Did he take any notice of the reason? It was spelt out in black and white, but all that explaining still had not got through to him. He didn't want to hear Anne prattling on to him, so he didn't bother with supper, he went straight to bed.

The next morning Anne was waiting for him to come to breakfast, she hadn't finished with him yet. "Where did you get to last night? We didn't finish our conversation. Are you going to treat our children as you have John? If so, don't bother coming to my bed ever again," she told him in anger. "John has the 'Irish curse', look at his red hair," he said. "But your mother was Irish, perhaps our children will have the same. It is in your bloodline, you are the carrier of the Irish gene. You can't take that out on innocent children. The red hair is because of you, Charles." "Don't ever say that again, Anne. I am English, not Irish. Everything Irish left here when my mother took her Irish brood with her!" Charles shouted. "No, Charles, your Irish blood will be with you for life, get used to it. I have accepted the fact that your Irish blood will run through our children, it doesn't worry me. If we have red-haired children, so be it. Be a man and accept who you are." This was the turning point. He lost his temper and dragged Anne through to her bedroom and ripped her clothes off. He would show her what sort of man he was.

7

The Meeting of the Irish

George and John were crossing the Irish Sea, and were nearly in Ireland. John was so excited, at last he was going to meet his grandmother Mary. He had dreamt of her many times, he even felt he knew her already. George had written to her and told her all about John's sad life, and the promise he had made to Elizabeth before she died. He had to carry out her last wish. Mary was going to be on the wharf to meet them. "Look, George, we are nearly there!" yelled John, as they came near the land. They stood on the deck, and George put his arms around John. "Thank you for bringing me to Ireland, I am so happy. I want you to be my new father, George." "I would love to be your father, John, but you already have a father. I know he has not treated you as his son, but one day he will want you, just you wait and see!" "Look, George, there are a lot of people waving to us," said an excited John.

They stood on the deck until the ship tied up at the wharf. As they walked down the gangway, they had to show their tickets before they could step on Irish soil. As they began to walk along the wharf a lady came running up to John and took him in her arms. "My darling boy, look at you, you are a true Irish lad, it is as if Joseph has been given back to us," she cried, holding on to him, not wanting to let him go. John cried alongside her, this he knew was his grandmother Mary, his heart told him so. Standing beside her was a man who she introduced as Grandad Connor. John could see tears in his eyes as he looked at him. His thoughts were the same as Mary's; their Joseph had come back to them. He shook John's hand, then hugged him. "Welcome to Ireland, John." "This is George, he was father's butler, he has been my only friend while at boarding school, he looked after me," said a proud John. "Hello, George, how can we thank you for looking after our grandson. You are most welcome to come and stay with us," said Mary. "Thank you but no, I will stay at the inn. You spend time with John. God knows he needs to be loved and accepted."

George felt he had betrayed Charles's family, so he couldn't stay with them. They drove in the carriage back to Cork and stayed in an inn for the night. The next morning, they all drove on to Drinagh where they booked George into the inn. Mary thanked him for writing to her and letting her know that she had a grandson and that he was being treated badly. She felt deep down for this child, as she knew the nature of his father. To think he would be disowned because of his red hair, such a petty crime. She asked George to come for supper one night and meet all the family; this he agreed upon. John hugged George goodbye. "Thank you, my best friend," he told him. This brought more tears to Mary's and Connor's eyes; fancy the butler being his only friend.

Then they went on their way to Curraghnaloughra, where Mary and Connor lived. John chatted all the way, he was so excited. "You know, Grandmother Mary, I have dreamed about you for five years. My mother made George promise to bring me to meet you, this has been our secret all this time. She told me you would love me, just as she still does." These were words from the mouth of an eleven-year-old boy. "Of course, we love you, John, you are very special to us. We didn't know about you until we received the letter from George, but we are together at last. We are kindred spirits who have been reunited, never to be parted, we are so proud of you," Mary told him. John hugged her. "I love you already, Grandmother Mary," he whispered. They drove the rest of the way home in each other's arms. Darkness was setting in and John had had a big day, so when they arrived, they had a bite of supper, then he asked to go to bed, as his eyes kept falling asleep. Both Mary and Connor kissed him goodnight; this had not happened since his mother had left him. Mary stayed and tucked him in, then sat on his bed and rubbed his forehead until he dropped off to sleep.

Mary and Connor both shed tears as they thought of the little boy lying in bed. What had he been through? Especially when they thought of the privileged life his father had, why would he treat his own child with such contempt? Of course, they knew the answer, when they saw the Irish hair. But this wasn't his fault, he was only a child. "You know, Mary, God has punished Charles, he has given us what Charles took from us, our Joseph!"

Connor said through his tears. "What a terrible life Elizabeth must have had, when she made George promise to bring John to us, she loved him. To think that is all the love he has known in his eleven years of life, oh, apart from his best friend, George. How sad! I met George on the morning I left the Rothchild estate, he seemed a pleasant young man. I wonder why he finished with Charles." Would she ever know the truth? This is what her daughter Rose had been hiding from her all these years.

Mary had arranged a family meeting when she received the letter from George, telling them what was happening on the estate and that Charles had a son who he had put in boarding school since the age of five. He had not even brought him home for the holidays, so he had lived there for the five years. The family were shocked to hear of this, and their hatred for Charles deepened further. It just didn't happen in this family; every family member was special. This, of course, made them more interested in meeting John and wanting to care for him as one of their own. They were excited; here was a young lad in need of so much love.

This morning John climbed out of bed, he felt happy; what his mother had told him about his grandmother Mary was all true. She loved him and he loved her back. As he entered the dining room Mary came over to him and kissed him on the cheek. "Did you sleep well, John?" "That's the best bed, the best one I have ever slept in," he told her. "That's good to hear. What would you like for breakfast?" "Oh, I just have porridge at school," he answered. "What about some bacon and eggs?" His eyes lit up; bacon and eggs, fancy having all this for breakfast. "Yes, please, you are so kind, Grandmother Mary," he said as he looked at her. She was a nice-looking lady with lovely red hair. "We have the same colour hair, "he told her. "So do all your cousins who you are going to meet today. They will love you," said Mary. "Father said I had the 'Irish curse', that is why he probably doesn't like me, but why, you have the 'Irish curse' and you are so kind." "Oh John, don't ever think of it as the 'Irish curse'. It is what we Irish call the 'Irish blessing'. We Irish are proud of our red hair, that is why we are Irish," Mary told him. "But father told me he wanted an English son, so he has married Anne. She is nice, she asked me down for the holidays as a surprise for father," then he went on to tell what happened. Tears filled Mary's eyes. How did she have such a cruel son? Thank God Albert never lived to see all this, he would have been disgusted. "Never mind, my darling, we will give you all the happiness you deserve," she told John. Connor came in from his workshop and sat and had breakfast with Mary and John. "What do you do, Grandad Connor?" he asked. Connor told him he had a workshop and he fixed broken farm equipment, in fact anything that was broken. "Can I come and help you in your big shed?" he asked. "Yes, you can be my helper, I would like that." So as soon as they finished their breakfast they both left for the workshop. John took Connor's hand and they walked together to the shed. Mary saw this from the window and knew Connor would be thinking this was his beloved Joseph with him again. He had never got over losing him. This thought brought more tears to Mary's eyes. It was John's father who took Joseph's life; now they were repaid with his son. How could they ever let him go back to boarding school? Mary knew in her heart he belonged to their family. The only thing English about John was his speech, the rest of him was Irish through and through.

After lunch Rose and Brendon and their family, along

with the twins and their families, arrived at Mary's, so it was a meeting of all the cousins. John had never seen so many red-haired children; they all looked just like him, they were his family. All the kids ran off together, pulling John along with them. When he was out of earshot, Mary told her children that John had been told by his father that he was the 'Irish curse', and that was why he didn't want anything to do with him. They were horrified, but they knew what their half-brother was capable of, they had experienced his spiteful behaviour as they were growing up. "Mother, what happened that George finished at the estate?" asked Rose. "I don't really know, but he is coming to supper one night, perhaps he will tell us," said Mary. "He did say he took a gardener's position at John's boarding school, just to look after him. I asked him to come and stay but he wanted to stay at the inn." The afternoon flew by, the children were away doing their thing, then they came back and everyone played ball. There was laughter aplenty, John had never had so much fun. This was a new world to him and he was loving every moment. "I am so lucky to have so many cousins. I didn't know I had any until now," he said proudly.

Everyone stayed for supper, it was one big happy family. When Mary tucked John into bed, he looked at her. "Mother told me she would always love me. I miss her. She died, so did our baby. You know, Grandmother Mary, she knew you and I would love each other, that's why she told George the secret she didn't want father to know." "Your mother would be proud of you, John. You have suffered at the hands of your father, you are so young to have experienced all this heartache. We all love you here, you have brought so much joy to our hearts, you will never know how much, but one day I will tell you a story that will explain why. But for now, this is another secret, our secret," Mary told him. John's eyes were slowly closing so Mary stroked his forehead till he dropped off to sleep.

Rose decided to pay George a visit at the inn one afternoon while she was in town. She was given his room number so she knocked on his door. "Hello, George, I'm Rose, Charles's half-sister." "Hello, Rose," George replied, wondering why she had come to see him. "Tell me, why did you leave the estate? Don't be alarmed, I knew you were Charles's lover. I am the only family member who knows this, it is a secret I have kept. Please tell me why you left." "When I saw how cruel Lord Charles was to John, especially when he put him in boarding school the day he turned five, just after he lost his mother, it broke my heart. When he completely ignored his own son, that was the end. I felt for John, like he was my own son. Elizabeth was a lovely mother to John and I made a promise to her, which I have now kept. I left Lord Charles a letter explaining why I left, and I have had no contact with him since," explained George. Rose reached across and took his hand. "Thank you, George, you are well rid of Charles, he is a bully. Your life with him would have been one of use and abuse. He has caused such sadness in our family. Find yourself someone deserving of you, you are a good person." "Thank you, Rose, but how did you know about us?" he asked. "At Charles's twenty-first, one of his friends left a letter under their pillow addressed to me and it explained his sexual preference. I was shocked but I kept it to myself, I didn't want mother to know as he had caused her so much grief. Please come to supper one night with our family, mother would like that, as she feels indebted to you." "Yes, that would be nice, thank you, Rose, for keeping our secret from your family."

The night George came for supper all the families were there. After they had eaten, the children all went to another room and left the adults to hold a meeting. What was going to happen to John? No-one wanted him to go back to boarding school. They asked George what he thought. "John gets on well with the kids at school. If he was taken away and Lord Charles found out, he would punish him. I would suggest he be left there until he turns fifteen, then it would be his choice. Perhaps if you could pay for him to come to Ireland in his holidays, it would give him comfort, knowing he was wanted and loved." "Thank you, George, we would love to keep him here with us, but we must do what is best for him. We all know what Charles is capable of; John can't suffer any more. Is everyone happy with these decisions?" asked Mary. They all agreed, but it would be sad to say goodbye to him, especially for Connor, as he saw in John what he envisaged his Joseph to be like. He had spent most of his time in the shed with Connor, helping him with repairs; he was his right-hand man. John felt important helping Connor. For the first time in his life he felt what it was like to be wanted.

This was John's last night in Ireland. Mary and Connor explained to him they would love him to come and live with them, but until he was fifteen he had to do what his father had arranged for him. They asked him to come to Ireland for all his school holidays, if he wanted to. "I would love to live here, but I know I cannot, because of father. To come for all my holidays would make me so happy. We won't tell father, this will our secret. Now I have another secret," he said with a smile. He loved secrets because they were all happy ones.

8

Coming Up Fifteen

John had one school holiday left before he turned fifteen. He had received a letter from Anne, asking for him to come back to the estate to meet his two half-sisters, who were aged four and three. She had talked it over with his father and he knew he was coming home. Because it was his last holidays before he went to Ireland to live with his grandparents, he decided to accept Anne's invitation, not that his father knew of his future plans, neither would he be told. It was another secret, but this was the best one of all! He would miss George, but he had persuaded John to take this opportunity, to go to Ireland and live among family that loved him. Nothing was ever going to change at the estate. Besides, George had met someone whom he was going to live with, so it was better that John be gone, so there was no embarrassment to anyone. He would always think of John as his son, and would write to him often. Perhaps when John got a little older, George hoped he could explain to him about his sexuality, but not now.

John was on the train to Oxshott to meet his half-sisters. He liked Anne but he did wonder how his father would treat him, not that it mattered any more. He had grown into a strapping teenager; he had taken up sports, which helped build up his muscles. As the train pulled into the station, he saw Anne and two little girls standing on the platform. He couldn't believe his eyes; the girls both had red hair, just like his. How did his father accept this? As he alighted from the train Anne ran up to him and put her arms around him. "Gosh, John, you have filled out, what a fine lad you are. Come and meet your sisters, Sarah and Lucy. Girls, this is your brother." The two girls looked at him and smiled. "How old are you?" one of them asked. "I am nearly fifteen," answered John proudly. "Come, we will drive to the estate. Do you want to take the reins, John?" asked Anne. "Yes, please, could I?" Anne gave him the reins and he sat up front and drove them back to the estate. As he pulled up in front of the home, there was his father standing by the stables. He pulled the horses to a stop, then jumped down and helped Anne and the girls alight from the carriage. Where did he learn to handle the horses and carriage? Charles asked himself. He certainly hadn't taught him. "Who taught you all this?" he asked. "I have learnt a lot of things, father. I have had good teachers, there are people who care for me." "Come with us, John!" yelled the girls as they tugged at him pulling him away with them.

Charles stood in disbelief. He was surprised to see that John had grown into such a strong lad. Anne noticed Charles looking at his son. "I hope you feel ashamed of yourself for the way you have treated John. The Irish curse will never leave you, Charles, it will be in any child you father. This is your penance for the hatred that lies within, you will never be rid of it. Your English son is only a dream. John is your reality and you have shunned him. I wonder what he really thinks of you. If you have hopes of this child in my belly being a son, an English one at that, may you get your wish, because there will be no more." Anne had had enough of his selfishness and his expectations, none of which had been met. She could do no more; she had given him two children with a third on the way, still he was not happy. She hadn't produced what he wanted, thus now deciding she never wanted him to bed her again. This was her last child. She loved her little girls but Charles showed very little love towards them. He did speak to them, more than what he had done with John. What of the next child? Would it suffer the same fate if it was born with the 'Irish curse'? Anne was disappointed with her life. She had come from a wealthy family and married Charles for betterment, but instead she felt belittled, it was as if she was a failure in all that she did. She couldn't find one redeeming feature about her husband, even his bedside manner was that of one who was on a mission and once performed, he left the scene.

One day Anne was grizzling about something that needed to be fixed on her carriage, would Charles please do something about it. "What is wrong?" enquired John. She took him out to the stables and showed him the problem. "I know how to fix that, I'll do it right now for you." So, he found the necessary tools and worked on it until it was mended. In the background, well out of sight, stood Charles. He watched as John worked away on the carriage, he seemed to know what he was doing.

Where did he learn these skills? he wondered. When John finished, he asked Anne if anything else needed seeing too. She lined up another couple of jobs for him to do. What an adaptable lad, she thought. The girls stayed in the stables with John, watching him at work. "Who showed you how to do that?" asked Sarah. "My Grandfather Connor in Ireland, he has a big workshop. I work with him in the school holidays, he has taught me so many things." "Have you been to Ireland?" asked Lucy. "Yes, many times," answered John. "What's it like there?" "I love it, my grandparents love me," he told them. "Father said we have the 'Irish curse' with our red hair," the girls told John. "Red hair is not an 'Irish curse', it is an 'Irish blessing'. Grandmother Mary told me that, she is Irish. She is your grandmother too, she would love you girls," John told them, knowing this to be true. She loved everything Irish.

That night at the dining table while they were having supper, one of the girls told their father, "Father, we don't have the 'Irish curse', our red hair is an 'Irish blessing'. "Who told you that?" he bellowed. "John told us that, his grandmother Mary told him." "When have you been speaking with her?" He turned on John. Now was the time to let it all out. "For the past four years I have been going to Ireland each school holidays to stay with Grandmother Mary and Grandfather Connor." "Don't mention that name Connor in this home ever again, he is not your grandfather. My father, Lord Albert, was your grandfather. Connor is nothing other than an Irish peasant, you are English," Charles told him. "Thank you, father, that is the first time you have thought of me as English, usually I am the 'Irish curse'," answered John. "How did you find them?" he asked. "George took me there. Mother asked him to take me to meet my grandmother Mary, he made this promise to her and he kept it." "What do you mean? How did you know where George was?" questioned Charles. "George has been a father to me all the time I was at boarding school, he has looked after me all those years, I love George." Just hearing the word love associated with George was all that was needed to set Charles off. "You didn't tell me about George, I didn't know where he went!" he yelled. "But you never talked to me, father. If you had, you would know all these things. George has been with me for nine years. He liked me, he said I was the son he could never have." With this Charles rushed from the room, he had to get away. The tears were rolling down his face, the passion he felt for him was still there in his heart, it had never left him. And to think George had loved his son, when it should have been himself who he loved. Why did all these awful things happen to him? he asked himself.

The rest of the family were still at the table. "I think that is a lovely saying of your grandmother's, John, that red hair is an 'Irish blessing'. See, girls, you have learnt something special today, be proud of yourselves. Was George the man you met at the station last time you were here? Who is he?" asked Anne. "George was father's private butler for many years, but he was upset when father sent me to boarding school, so he left here to look after me. He was angry he sent me away so young, mother didn't want me to go, but then she died. Father was very sad when George left, but I wasn't allowed to tell father where he was. This was George and my secret." Anne wondered why this was a secret, it seemed strange. "It is good to see you stand up to your father, John. He can be a very strong-headed man. He has done wrong by you, and I think he may be hurting a little, for I have never given him the son he wants. Perhaps this baby will make him happy," said Anne as she patted her belly. Charles didn't come back to the table; no-one saw him for the rest of the night.

Next morning John took the girls into the woods to see the squirrels. They had never been there before, so they squealed with delight when they saw the little animals scramble up the trees, then sit with their tails hanging down like feather dusters. "This is fun, John, you are a good brother. Will you come back and live with us?" they both asked. "I'm going to live in Ireland soon, when I'm fifteen. I will go to college there, but father doesn't know yet. I have to tell him before I go back to school." "Do you think he will be angry?" asked Sarah. "Probably, but I have decided I want to live with Grandmother Mary and Grandfather Connor. They are nice people, they are your grandparents too. Perhaps one day you will meet them," said John. "Do you think father will take us?" "No, he has nothing to do with them. One day when you are older you might want to visit them on your own, I might still be there." "We hope you are, John, then we can see you again," they said.

John's stay at the estate had come to an end. Tomorrow he was leaving to go back to school. Tonight, they were having a family supper, and for once Charles even seemed happy. "John, I have enrolled you at my old college at the beginning of next term, where I want you to study law." "I'm sorry, father, but I have enrolled in a college in Ireland. I am going to study engineering." Charles jumped up from his chair in a rage. "You are my son, you will study in England, I am paying for your education!" he said as he banged his fists on the table. "I am going to live with my grandparents. Grandfather Connor has enrolled me in a very good college, where I can study engineering, that is what I want to do, not law," he told his father. This was the end, Charles came around and grabbed John and shook him. "I will not pay for your education in Ireland. Don't you ever talk of that peasant Irishman as your grandfather, he is not!" "I'm sorry, father, you had your chance with me but you never cared. I am going to Ireland when school finishes. I don't need your money; my grandparents are going to support me through college. Then I will probably work for Grandfather Connor to repay my debts," said John.

Charles was so upset. To think his mother was taking his son away from him, this was it. "If you go to Ireland, you will no longer be my son!" Charles yelled. Anne intervened: "Charles, he is your son, how can you be so cruel? Don't do this, you will regret these words." "Please, father, we love John, he is our big brother," cried the girls. "I have spoken, what is it, John, England or Ireland?" "I have chosen to go to Ireland. If this is the end of us, then there was never much there to hold us together. Mother was so right when she said my Irish grandmother would love me. We love each other," he told his father with such conviction. "What your father has said, he speaks for himself, these are not my thoughts. I would love you for my son, you are a great boy, John. Sadly, he has dreams and none of them have come to fruition, but still he holds on to them. The girls and I will write to you," said a sad Anne. On this note, John excused himself and said goodnight to Anne and the girls, but bypassed his father. He expected him to be upset, but never disown him. He went to bed with a heavy heart.

This morning there were sad goodbyes. The girls hugged John and cried as they did so, telling him they would miss him. Anne was brokenhearted, her husband was not the man she thought he was, but this she had found out too late. She had married for position, not for love, but gain had not made her happy. This was the last time she would carry a child fathered by Charles. He was aggressive in the bedroom; to him it was a duty to be performed and got over as quickly as possible. She took John in her arms and hugged him with such passion, he was a great lad and deserved better than what he was dealt. "Your mother would be proud of you, John. Follow her wishes, go to your Irish grandparents, to where you will be loved, this you deserve. One day your father will regret his words to you, but then it will be up to you. Goodbye, dear boy, please write to the girls and me, we will write back," said a tearful Anne. "Take care, John." Then the tears flowed. Charles had left for work early, he didn't want to face his son. The gardener drove John to the station. As he waited for the train to arrive, he saw his father at the end of the platform walking towards him. He stood and faced him like a man. "Tell George I want him to come back," then he turned and walked away. John thought he had come to say goodbye, but no, this was not to be. Why would he want George back? He couldn't understand this.

9

The Family Grows

Anne was on tenterhooks. Could she give Charles the son he so wanted? He talked so much about his English son, the heir to the Rothchild estate. There had been no mention of John since he left the estate six months ago. Anne had received a letter from him and he had started at the college in Ireland. He was happy living with his grandparents and was enjoying the engineering course he had enrolled for. The girls talked about their big brother all the time, even dragging Anne into the woods to watch the squirrels. She had never ventured into the woods before, so it was an outing for her. The girls had happy memories of their time in there with John. He was never mentioned in front of his father.

Charles even seemed to take a little interest in Anne, now that the birth was close, but it was having a son he cared for most. This was going to be Albert II, the next lord of the Rothchild estate. Anne went into labour early one morning, so it was all go. Charles ran to the stables and hitched the horses to the carriage. He had to get her to the hospital, there was to be no delay, this was an important day. The cook would attend to the girls when they woke up. On their arrival at the hospital Anne was taken straight into a ward as her pains were increasing. Charles was shown to the waiting room. The wait seemed like hours; he wished Anne would hurry up, he wanted news of his son! Much later the nurse came through. "Congratulations, Lord Charles, you have twins, a daughter and a son." He couldn't wait to see his son but he was told the babies were being taken to a special unit as they were both very small. Could he come back later? He never enquired about Anne; he had his son, that was all he needed to know, hoping that the 'Irish curse' had not been put on him.

He was so happy he went back to the estate and took the top off a bottle of whisky. One small celebrity glass turned into several more, until he lay on the settee totally out to it and went to sleep. When he woke, it was in the middle of the night and he was in total darkness. What had happened? Then he remembered he had a son. He couldn't go to the hospital now, he would have to wait until the morning. It was mid-morning before Charles surfaced. His head was spinning, the empty whisky bottle lay on the floor; no wonder his head was hurting!

When he arrived at the hospital, he was met at the front desk by the nurse, who asked him to come to a private waiting room, as the doctor wanted to speak to him. "Lord Charles, your babies are very small. There is a problem with your son, he is poorly, we are worried about him.

Go to your wife, she needs you, she had a hard labour." Charles was upset, all he wanted to do was see his son. "Can I see my son first?" he asked. The doctor took him through to see the babies. There lay two tiny souls, both with dark hair, the 'curse' was gone. He now had his little Albert. The doctor took him through to see Anne who was just waking. She looked at Charles. "You have a son and a daughter, have you seen them?" she asked. "Yes, but they are very tiny. The doctor said Albert was very poorly. Nothing must happen to him, he is my son and heir." "But what about your daughter?" asked Anne. "It is Albert I am worried about. I already have two daughters; my son must be saved." "But that is cruel Charles," whispered Anne. "I will sacrifice my daughter, if it means saving my son, my son must live." The master had spoken. Anne had heard enough; any feelings for Charles died in that moment. She would be his wife in name only. She closed her eyes pretending to be asleep. She had heard enough, wishing that this conversation had never taken place. How could anyone be so cruel? But she had seen it with John, it would never go away. All Charles worried about was the 'Irish curse' and producing a son. Would all his wrongdoings catch up with him one day? Was penance lying in wait?

That night back at the estate, Charles had supper with his daughters, telling them he now had a son. "But we have a sister too," said Sarah. Charles was not interested in another daughter, although this one had dark hair. The cook took the girls to the kitchen to help her, as she knew how short-tempered Lord Charles was with his daughters. He went to the cabinet and took out another bottle of whisky. This was to wet the head of his English-born son, his heir! This pleased him immensely. Then his thoughts drifted back to the days when George was part of his life.

He loved him and still did, if only he hadn't left. But to find out he left to look after John at boarding school for all those years hurt him so much. He felt John had stolen George from him, and for this he would never be forgiven. He went to the drawer, unlocked it and lifted out George's letter, which he held close to his heart. He could never forget him. Secretly he hoped he would come back, but time was marching on. It was a long shot, but he held on to hope that one day they would again be lovers. The alcohol painted a rosy picture!

Just on dusk today the housekeeper's husband had come to collect her as there had been a family tragedy, so she brought the girls through for Charles to look after. "I haven't prepared supper yet, but I have to leave, you will have to look after the girls," she told Charles. She was a little worried as she saw the half bottle of whisky on the table, but she could do nothing, she had to go. "What are you drinking, father?" Lucy asked. "It is none of your business," he told her. "We are hungry, can you get us some supper?" "No, I'm busy, make yourself something," he told them. Then he poured himself another drink, and went back to his reminiscing over George. The girls decided to make their father a cup of tea, so they filled a pot with water and put it on the cast iron stove, as the cook had the stove all fired up when she was called away. The girls watched the water as it boiled away, then Sarah decided to lift it down. She grabbed the handle and it was hot so she let the pot go and boiling water splashed over Lucy's face and down her neck and chest.

Amid his reminiscing Charles heard a scream, so ran to the kitchen and there was Lucy screaming as the boiling water had scalded her. Sarah was crying, she had burnt her little sister. Charles tried to run to the stable to fetch the carriage but he stumbled several times, the whisky had taken effect, and the screaming continued. When he eventually got the carriage to the front entrance he ran and picked up Lucy and put her in it. Sarah just stood overcome with grief. "Get in the carriage, girl!" he screamed at her. He drove like a madman to the hospital, panic had taken over. When he arrived, he carried her in as she was in terrible pain and crying. The nurse took one look at her and saw she needed a doctor right away. Then the stark realisation of having to tell Anne soon helped sober him up. The doctor was horrified when he saw the burns the little girl had received, asking Lord Charles how it happened. He administered pain relief and applied ointment to the burn areas. He said Lucy's face would be scarred for life, as would her neck and chest. She would spend many days in hospital so the nurses could apply the ointment and wait for the skin to repair. Infection was the next problem, which was why she couldn't go home.

Meanwhile Sarah had asked to see her mother. When Anne learned of the accident she was horrified. How did this happen? Where was the cook? Among her tears, Sarah tried to explain how it happened, that it was her fault. "Where was your father?" asked Anne. "He was drinking in the drawing room, he told us to get ourselves some supper." At that very moment Charles appeared, but Anne got in first. "You can't even be trusted to care for your children. How is Lucy?" "I'm sorry, Anne, Lucy is badly burned, she has been sedated. How is my son?" he asked. Anne could smell alcohol on his breath; she didn't answer him. She left her bed to go and see her daughter. A nurse helped her through to the ward where Lucy lay. She burst into tears, this was her child, her face and neck were blistered and badly inflamed. She sat on her bed and held her hand. Sarah had followed her and cuddled into her mother, all the time sobbing that this was all her fault. "Don't blame yourself, Sarah, it was an accident," Anne told her, knowing all the time with whom the blame lay!

Six months later the babies were settled in at the estate and Lucy had been released from hospital. Her upper body was still bandaged and these had to be changed every day, with new ointment applied to keep any infection at bay. Sarah was her full-time nurse as she still blamed herself for what happened to her sister. The babies were still small, they took a lot of caring for, and Anne was kept busy from daylight to dark. Charles spent more time at his law office, as every time he saw Lucy it reminded him that what happened that night was because of him. He enquired about his son every day, as he was still too small for him to handle, never about his daughter. He did at times feel a little remorseful about Lucy, but his son was more important than anyone in the household. He was his main concern. He got impatient when his daughter was doing well, as Albert didn't seem to be growing at the same rate as his sister. This upset Charles. Was he being fed properly? Was Anne favouring Jane over Albert? All these stupid thoughts were running through his head. He wanted a strong son, not a weak one! He had actually accused Anne of not looking after Albert. Why else was he so tiny when his sister was a much stronger baby? Anne reminded him of the doctor's words. "He was concerned about Albert's health right from the day he was born." But Charles would not take this on board. This was his English son and heir, surely nothing could be wrong with him?

These were turbulent times on the estate. Charles was lonely and had even made time to visit Anne at nights only to be turned away. She had a lot to forgive him for and as yet that hadn't happened. She received letters from John in Ireland, and these were a breath of fresh air. He was loving living with his grandparents and college was going well; in all he loved Ireland, he felt it was now his home. He had plenty of cousins and they all loved him. He would go to church on Sundays and leave flowers on Joseph's grave. Who was Joseph? Anne wondered. She had never heard his name mentioned before; she would ask Charles. The girls would write little letters to John and put them in with their mother's. No-one spoke of him in front of their father.

One day Anne remembered to ask Charles who Joseph was. "Don't mention that name on this estate ever again. Who told you about him?" he asked angrily. "Your son John puts flowers on his grave each Sunday when he attends church," said Anne. "That's right, that Irish nobody would have put him up to that," scoffed Charles. "But who was he?" Anne asked again. "He was my older brother. Don't mention his name ever again," he said as he walked away. Anne left it at that, but next time she wrote to John, she would ask him what happened to Joseph. It had certainly hit a raw nerve with Charles; perhaps he was still in mourning for his brother?

Meanwhile in Ireland, Mary and Connor knew what was happening on the estate because of Anne and the girls' letters to John. He would read them to his grandparents. They were really upset to hear about Lucy's accident, but even more concerned that she would be scarred for life. How sad for the young girl! Mary made up her mind that she would like Lucy to come to Ireland one day, to see if there was anything that could be done for her. She asked John to put this in his next letter to Anne, as she knew nothing ever got back to Charles. These children were her grandchildren and she cared for them. Now that Charles had his new English son, he was on top of the world. At last he had his heir, but then he already had one in John. But the 'Irish curse' had robbed him of his rightful title. Mary wondered how he was going to overcome the fact that the title went to the eldest son regardless of any likes or dislikes. Could Charles big-note himself enough to change the law that had stood for many years? Was he that powerful? Mary knew that peerage had a big pull in English society. One thing for sure, no harm would come to John while he lived with them in Ireland.

Every Sunday, when they visited Joseph's grave, they were reminded of the gun incident between him and Charles. The lies that were told, until many years later in the heat of the moment, when it was revealed callously by Charles that he pulled the trigger on Joseph, which left the way clear for him to become a lord when his father died. John had taken Joseph's place in Connor's heart. He was all Connor ever wanted in a son, someone who was practical and kind, like himself. He often wondered how Charles could father such a lovely son, but then, how did Mary produce a self-centred upstart like Charles? There was no explanation for that either!

10

How the Years Fly By

Five years had passed and the twins were turning five. Would Albert be shipped off to boarding school, as was John? The answer was no! Charles wanted him close, as he was still a weak little boy and needed all the right care to get him stronger. His sister Jane was fighting fit and a picture of health. Why, Charles asked himself, did she have to rob Albert of the health that was rightfully his? She should have been the weak one, not her brother. Charles didn't pay much attention to his daughter. She annoyed him, she was so robust and full of energy. Why was this so? he asked; justice had not been served.

One day the long-awaited letter from John arrived, explaining who Joseph was and what had happened to him. Anne was stunned to hear this awful story, especially that her husband had actually admitted in a moment of rage that he had shot Joseph so he could become the eldest son and therefore entitled to the peerage when his father died. Thus making him the lord of the Rothchild estate. But the irony was, it never belonged to Joseph, as he was not Lord Albert's son, he was Connor's son, so this was a senseless act, and an innocent child lost his life through the greed of his half-brother. To this day, this had not been revealed, not even Charles knew this. It was better left unmentioned, the suffering had been done, although Connor never forgave Charles for this selfish act. He had lost his son, his best friend. Now the same scenario was happening in the next generation, only John being the eldest son was the one entitled to the peerage and the estate before Albert. What was Charles thinking? Anne knew in her own mind that because John had the 'Irish blessing' like her two eldest daughters, they were disadvantaged. She loved John as if he were her own son, he was gentle and kind. The girls thought of him as their big brother.

Little Albert was about to start school with his sister Jane. Charles told Jane she was to look after him and make sure nothing happened to him, she was his caregiver. This put pressure on her. Anne asked Charles not to be so hard on Jane but this was ignored, she had been told what was expected of her. Each day her father reminded her of her duties, so this made her paranoid. She was afraid to let him out of sight in case something happened to him. She couldn't make friends in the playground as she was always attending to Albert. One day he fell over and came home with a cut to his knee. When Charles saw this, he sought out Jane and took privileges away from her. She cried, as she didn't mean for it to happen to her brother. "You be more careful, don't let this happen again," her father warned her. Anne was angry. Why was all this focus on Albert? Jane had to be allowed to do her own thing, she was just a child, the same as Albert.

It wasn't long before Albert was smart enough to sense he was the superior being here in this home, so he started to demand things. Jane's life became a living hell as he ran to his father with every little lie he could think of to get Jane in trouble, for which she was punished. Although she was the healthier of the twins, her self-worth plummeted as her brother's demands grew. One day she was so angry with him, she shoved him and he fell over. He lay on the ground screaming until his father came running. "What happened, Albert?" "Jane pushed me over," he told his father. "Right, my girl, get to your room and don't come down for supper." Jane ran to her room in tears. She hated her brother, he was spoilt rotten. Anne had witnessed this incident, but her verbal contributions were disregarded by Charles. He could see no wrong in Albert. Was this history repeating itself down the next generation? This was an exact replica of Charles's younger life. Was Albert going to turn out like his father?

Today Charles decided to go to his office and catch up on some work. It was the weekend and the children were playing around the stables. They had been told not to go near the horses, but today, this rule was going to be broken. Lucy saw something shiny in the hay at the back of the stable so she decided to see what it was. As she was wriggling under the stable door, Albert appeared beside her, thus frightening the two horses who reared up and kicked out at Albert. He let out a yell, which caused the horses to panic thus trampling on him and Lucy. Sarah and Jane ran to the home to get their mother. Anne came running over to the stables to find Lucy and Albert lying under the horses. She had to get the horses out before she could get to the children, so she unhinged the door and the horses bolted. It was only then she was able to get to them. Albert was lying still, there was no movement from him, but Lucy was moving and crying. She lifted her out and went back to attend to Albert, but she couldn't wake him. She was frightened to lift him; he was still breathing, but was unconscious. Anne needed to get a doctor to Albert, so left Sarah and Jane to sit with him while she put Lucy in the carriage and drove to the hospital. She left Lucy to be attended to by a nurse and told a doctor what had happened, so he came back with her to the estate.

When the doctor saw Albert's motionless body lying on the hay, he was shocked. He examined him and found his body was covered in bruises where the horse had trampled on him. He would have to get him to the hospital straight away, as he thought he would certainly have internal injuries, perhaps even internal bleeding. Between Anne and the doctor, they managed to lift Albert into the carriage. Anne sat with him while the doctor drove to the hospital. When they arrived, Albert was taken straight to a ward so he could be examined. Meanwhile Lucy had been attended to by a nurse and apart from bruising she was relatively unscathed, but her tears would not stop flowing. What was her father going to say if anything happened to Albert? The girls all knew their brother was the one most loved by their father. They were his keepers, the ones who were meant to look out for him at all times. Nothing was ever to happen to him, now this?

Lucy's injuries were minor compared to Albert's, but she would be sore for many days until the bruising all came out. She was so lucky she wasn't kicked in the face where all her scar tissue was still mending. The left side of her face and neck were quite disfigured, but being young it didn't seem to matter, but this would change when she reached her teenage years. Albert was the big worry. He was still unconscious, but this was a good thing, until they found out the extent of his injuries. Now Anne had to break the news to Charles!

When Charles was told Albert was in hospital, he erupted, "Where were the girls, they were meant to be looking after him, protecting him from any sort of danger?" He didn't at this moment know what had happened, otherwise all hell would have broken loose. Instead he left his office and hurried to the hospital leaving Anne trailing behind him. He had to see his Albert. When he saw his son, he sat and cried. "What has happened to you, Albert? Anne, what happened to him?" he asked. All Anne could do was tell the truth. "Wait till I get my hands on that girl!" he yelled in rage. "But Charles, it was an accident, she has suffered too, don't be too hard on her," she begged. "I will not have her in my home, she is off to boarding school, I will arrange it as soon as possible." "But she was hurt too, please don't send her away, she has been through so much," cried Anne. Charles told Anne to leave, as he wanted to spend time alone with Albert. As yet the full extent of Albert's injuries was not known, it was still a waiting game.

Anne picked Lucy up from the hospital and drove her back to the estate so she could be with her sisters. Thank god Charles didn't know she was there. They all knew there were going to be consequences because of what had happened to Albert. Anne reassured her daughters that whatever happened she loved them and would stand by them. What had happened was an accident and because they were young kids, they didn't think of the consequences when making silly decisions. This was all part of growing up. Would Charles look at it the same way as Anne? The answer to this would be a definite no. He didn't come home for supper and when Anne went to bed, he had still not returned. The next morning at breakfast he was not present, so she assumed he must have spent the night at the hospital.

Anne decided to take the carriage to the hospital to see how Albert was, but decided to leave the girls with the housekeeper, as she was concerned as to how he would react to them. It was better not to be displayed in public. Charles barely spoke to Anne. They sat together by Albert's bed, as the doctor was going to report to them shortly. Albert had still not stirred since his accident; he lay unconscious, looking pale and sick. The nurse came and asked them to come through to the doctor's room. The news was not good, he had suffered internal injuries and would be a sick boy for a very long time. It would take many months for him to recover, and then nothing could be guaranteed at the end of his recovery period. It was still a matter of wait and see. Tears ran down Charles's face. Anne had never seen him shed tears until today, but then so much hinged around this little boy, the whole future of the Rothchild estate. She wondered what consequences would befall Lucy.

That night she sat and wrote a letter to John, explaining what had happened and how she feared for Lucy. Charles had made it quite clear that she was not to live at home, but to send her to boarding school would be wrong, she would suffer even more. She would be a target for bullying with her scarred face. Could he talk to Grandmother Mary and ask her if Lucy could come and live with them until things settled down at the estate? She was her grandchild, surely she would love her and keep her safe. Anne talked this over with Lucy, this was their secret, no-one else would know. "I would love to see John again and he talks as if Grandmother Mary is a nice lady. I will miss you, mother and my sisters," she said through her tears. But she knew that her life at the estate, because of what happened to Albert, would be unbearable, as this was all her fault. Her father would hate her, and if the unimaginable happened, that Albert never recovered, then what? She had accepted her fate!

Several weeks had passed and Albert lay in hospital, still very sick. Charles spent most of his time by his son's side, so he was rarely seen on the estate. He did, however, mention to Anne that he was going to arrange a boarding school for Lucy. Thankfully Anne had received a letter from Ireland and it was written by Mary herself. She told Anne she would be delighted to have Lucy come to stay with them, she couldn't bear the thought of her being sent off to boarding school away from her family. She mentioned a date that she would cross the Irish Sea and be at the train station in London. If Anne could put her on the train, she would meet her at the London station.

11

Lucy's New Life

The day had arrived, no-one except Anne and Lucy knew what was happening. They had packed her clothes during the night and hid the trunk in the carriage. Anne drove her to the station and put her on the train. She cried as she hugged her daughter goodbye, but she knew she couldn't stay at the estate, her life would be hell. Mary would love her, as she carried the 'Irish blessing', which would be accepted by the Irish. She stood on the platform and waved until the train disappeared out of sight, tears streaming from her eyes. When would she see her daughter again? What had happened to her high-society life as Lady Rothchild, the life she had chosen above all else? All it had brought was one problem after another, but this was by far the worst, to have to send her daughter away from her home. The one that had suffered so much, it didn't seem fair, but Charles was the master of his estate, she was merely a chattel. She would tell Sarah and Jane tonight, but it would have to remain a secret among the three of them. She would tell Charles she was staying with a friend for a while, that was if he even noticed she was not there. She decided not to mention anything until Charles brought it up.

Lucy sat on the train thinking ahead. What was her new life going to be like? She was happy with the thought of not being ignored by her father any more, as it was making her very sad. Then her thoughts went to Albert. She should have told him off, and not let him follow her under the stable door, but she never thought of the consequences, they were only kids, it was a spur-of-the-moment decision. Then she asked herself, What would Grandmother Mary look like? She had never seen a photo of her, there were no photos of her on the estate. As the train pulled into the London station, all she could see was faces everywhere. Which one belonged to her grandmother? She alighted from the train with her trunk and waited on the platform. Suddenly she felt her trunk being taken from her. She looked around and there was a beautiful-looking lady standing beside her. "Hello, Lucy, I am your grandmother Mary," she said. She took Lucy in her arms and held on to her, thus bringing tears from Lucy. She cried as she clung to her grandmother; she felt an immediate warmth flowing from her, the same warmth that came from her mother. "Hello, grandmother, you look lovely, you have the 'Irish blessing'. Look at your red hair, it's the same as mine. Father told us it was the 'Irish curse', but John told us you said it was an 'Irish blessing'." "Come, my child, we will talk later. I have booked us into an inn for the night, then we will cross the Irish Sea in the morning." Lucy took her grandmother's hand and hung on for grim death. She didn't want to lose her, she had just found her. Mary looked at this dear soul who was but eight years old, with scars down the left side of her face. They continued down her neck; how far did they go? she wondered. John had explained to his grandmother how this had happened. It all came back to Charles, who took no interest in his two eldest children and told them to get their own supper.

Mary could not believe how cruel Charles was towards his own flesh and blood, simply because of the colour of their hair; he didn't deserve any children. They didn't deserve to be shunned, they were the innocent ones in all this. "Lucy, tell me, what do you know about Ireland?" asked Mary. "I know nothing, it was not allowed to be mentioned in our home. Father hated everything Irish, that is why he didn't love John, Sarah or myself. When the twins came along things were different, they didn't have red hair. But Jane had a terrible life, as father told her she had to look after Albert every minute of every day. She was like a slave to him, she hated Albert as he was spoilt. It is sad, mother loves all her children, but not father. If anything happens to Albert, father will hate me more, I will never be allowed to go home, he would not let me back," Lucy said as tears streamed down her face. "You poor child, you are too young to have suffered as you have. We will love you as one of our own family," said Mary as she took her in her arms and held her close. How did I have such a cruel son? she asked herself.

The next morning, they caught the ferry to Ireland. Lucy hung on to Mary's hand, never letting it go. This was all new to her and she felt a little afraid. It reminded Mary of her young life, when she left her family home to find a better life in London, but then she was nineteen years; Lucy was only eight years old. Now years later, she was helping her granddaughter to find none other than love, a little word with so much meaning. They sat on the ferry and talked nonstop, with Mary catching up on what was going on in Lucy's life. When the ferry docked in Ireland, they waited until it was cleared for them to leave, and as they walked down the gangway, there waiting for them was Connor. Mary gave him a kiss and then she introduced him to Lucy. "Lucy, this is your grandfather Connor." "Hello, Grandfather Connor, I'm pleased to meet you," she said as she shook his hand. He looked at this young girl with the scarred face and felt deep down in his heart for her. He knew Mary would love and protect her, as he would. They caught a carriage to Cork then booked into an inn for the night, before their journey to Curraghnaloughra tomorrow. Lucy shared a room with her grandparents and they both kissed her goodnight and tucked her in; she felt special! It had been a big day.

As they arrived at her grandparents' house, Lucy couldn't believe the beautiful colour in the paddocks, as the wheat was ready to yield. The land was covered in gold, and this made her feel happy. "Grandmother, this is a lovely welcome, it looks like the sun has painted the land for me," she said with sincerity. Suddenly there were people everywhere, this was her family, they were all there to welcome her to her new home. Lucy was bewildered by all these new faces, but they were her cousins and uncles and aunts. Then she spotted John and ran to him. "You have grown into a man now, John, gosh you look older, look at your Irish beard." Everyone laughed at Lucy's comments. John hugged her. He was sad to see how scarred she was, as he remembered her as a pretty little girl. "Did you read my letters?" she asked him. "Yes, Lucy, I loved getting letters from my family. You will love it here, this is my home now. I love Ireland and its people." "You are my big brother, yes, I will be happy here. Look at everyone, they all have the 'Irish blessing'. We are Irish, John, father was right," replied Lucy. Everyone knew the story of the 'Irish curse' that Charles had bestowed upon his red-haired children, but they all knew he was a pompous aristocrat. The cousins took Lucy to show her which was her bedroom. Yes, she was going to like it here, she felt safe and she had lots of friends already. "You will come to school with us, Lucy, we will look after you," they told her. She had never had so many friends. This felt good, but she did miss her mother. She would write to her, but there would be so much to put on paper!

Back at the Rothchild estate, Alfred was still in hospital. He was not recovering very quickly from the trampling he received from the horses. His internal injuries were severe and because he was not a strong boy, his healing was taking longer than what everyone expected. Charles spent most of his spare time sitting with his son, telling him of his peerage and that one day he would be lord of the Rothchild estate. This brought smiles to his face; even at a young age he had that bullying manner that accompanied many of the spoilt upper-class children. He had exerted these on his sisters, especially Jane, his twin, as his father had appointed her as his keeper and he tested her to the limit, knowing this was with his father's approval. She wasn't missing her brother; at last she found she had a life of her own. She had grown to dislike him, not that she wanted anything to happen to him, but not to have him home was pure bliss. Anne would take the girls to the hospital to see Albert when Charles was at his law office. Charles had not once asked about Lucy. It was as if she never existed in the first place. Did he even know she was no longer living at home? One day Albert asked, "Why doesn't Lucy come and visit me?" "She has gone to live with a friend. Your father blamed her for what happened to you," his mother told him. "It wasn't her fault. It was yours, Jane, you were meant to see that nothing happened to me," he hit back. "Albert, that is not fair, you cannot blame your sisters, you knew what you were doing was wrong," replied his mother. "But father told Jane she had to make sure no harm came to me," he snapped. With this, Jane ran from the room. She was so hurt. She would never come back and visit him, he was still horrible to her, even from his hospital bed. I hate him, she said to herself. Anne didn't stay long, she had to find Jane. She was disgusted with Albert's comments, he was a spoilt child, but this was all thanks to Charles. Sarah followed her mother and they both went to look for Jane. There she was, huddled under a tree in the hospital gardens crying her heart out. Sarah went and brought her back to the carriage and they drove home to the estate. "I will never go back to the hospital," she said through her tears. The girls missed Lucy, but they knew they could not mention her name in front of their father.

Charles had not come back to Anne's room since the twins were born. This suited her, as her dislike for him was growing. The only person in his life was Albert, his successor. The girls were totally disregarded; they, like Anne, had become mere chattels. She had seen this in the aristocracy; the men were the masters who ruled to their advantage. But John was not like this, he was more Irish than English, he was gentle and kind. She wished he was her son, but then realised, he was the boy he was because he was never spoilt or told he was of peerage breeding. His life had been one of sadness, but he had turned out to be a good lad, one that would make any mother proud. She was happy that he and Lucy were together, as they would form a bond, and realise they were both better off in Ireland, where they were loved, where their red hair was just part of everyday life.

The girls were having piano lessons; this was so the beautiful piano that sat in the drawing room would be put to use. It was Charles's wedding present to Elizabeth, his first wife, but it had not been played since her death. They were diligent students and practised every day, not that their father had heard them, as he was still spending most of his spare time at the hospital. One day Albert's recovery came to a halt, as an infection had brought on a fever, thus causing much concern. There was nothing that could be done for him, it was just a case of waiting until it passed. The days came and went but there was no improvement and he became gravely ill. "Please save him, he is my heir, nothing must happen to him," cried Charles, but could all the tears and pleading save Albert?

12

Dark Days Ahead

Lord Charles sat at Albert's bedside in his last hours. When the doctor announced he had passed away he didn't tell Anne, he wanted to grieve for his son by himself. This was his son and heir and now he was gone. Why did Albert have to go? Why couldn't it have been Lucy? She was of no significance, Charles said to himself. Where was she? He hadn't seen her about, but she would suffer, she was the cause of Albert's death. He sat grief-stricken until the nurse asked him to leave so she could do the final preparations. He drove back to his estate and sat in the carriage for hours, until Jane came out and saw her father crying. "What's happened, father?" she asked. "Albert, my son, he has gone," he cried. Jane ran to tell her mother. When Anne learnt of Albert's death, she gathered the girls and they huddled together. They left Charles to grieve on his own; his son was his whole life, now he had been taken from him. What is left? he asked himself, just girls, but what of John, his eldest son? Jane was sad that her brother had died, but she could see that life was going to be less complicated for her, at last she would have a life.

When Charles did eventually come back into the home, he went straight to Anne and asked where Lucy was. "Lucy hasn't lived here for several months now." "Where is she? She was the cause of Albert's death!" he yelled. "No, Charles, it was an accident, don't blame her," said Anne as she tried to calm him. But he had to deal with this the only way he knew and that was to hurt others. "But Albert was my son and heir, now I have no son." "You do have another son, Charles, and his name is John, in case you have forgotten," Anne reminded him. "I only ever had one son," he snapped back. Anne could see the rage in his eyes. He wasn't going to listen to her point of view, so she gathered the girls and they went into the drawing room. Sarah sat down at the piano and began to play. Charles heard the music and came storming through. "Stop playing that piano, it belongs to Elizabeth." Anne felt hurt, this was her home, Elizabeth was long gone. "You are hurting, Charles, as we all are, don't make things worse," she told him. With this he stalked off to his wing. Why wasn't George here to share his grief? He needed him at this moment. He had never given up on the thought he would come back. He went to the drawer and unlocked it and took out George's letter, clutching it to his chest; this was his only reminder of his lost love.

Today was Albert's funeral. Everyone knew how grief-stricken Lord Charles was and they felt for him. He sat beside Anne and the girls in church while the service was being taken. It was a sad day for the whole family, they had lost a son and brother. Anne and the girls did not go to the burial, as it was a cold damp day; they would take flowers up to the grave tomorrow. Lord Charles was receiving condolences from all the gentry and clients from his law practice, so he didn't spend much time with his family; they were not as important as all the others. Everyone came back to the Rothchild estate for drinks and hors d'oeuvres, so Anne and the girls were kept busy making tea for the ladies. Out of the blue Charles asked Sarah to play the piano. She was surprised. "Are you sure, father?" she asked. He waved his hand for her to play. He stood and listened. She played like Elizabeth. If only George were here with him, this brought back wonderful memories. Then it was all over, suddenly reality struck, and he remembered Albert. He instructed Sarah to stop playing, and he left the room.

Anne and the girls sat down to write to Lucy. She had to know that Albert had passed away, but what effect would it have on her? Charles had told her to her face that she was responsible for Albert's accident, and now would she feel the same about his death? Anne wondered if she should write to John and let him break it to Lucy. He was gentle, he would know how to handle it; yes, that is what she would do. She asked Sarah and Jane not to mention about Albert in their letters and explained why. In the letter they had received from Lucy, she told them she loved Ireland. Everyone she lived with was kind and loving, especially Grandmother Mary. She would cuddle her each night then tuck her in bed and sit and rub her forehead. She loved John; he would take her to visit her cousins, they were her best friends. This made Anne happy. She missed Lucy, but she realised life at the estate would be impossible for her, now that Albert was gone. She was sad to think Charles didn't know she was gone, he hadn't missed her. What would happen now that Charles didn't have his English son? Would he accept John, the rightful heir to the estate?

That night when Anne went to bed, she felt sad the way her life had panned out. What had happened? She was going to be the lady of the Rothchild estate throwing society parties and mixing with the elite, but this had never come to fruition. These dreams were gone! She had become like all other gentlemen's wives, a homebody who hadn't amounted to much. She would miss Albert, but now the girls' lives were going to be more liberated. Perhaps their father would notice them now? Anne often thought of Charles's mother, Mary. She had heard so much about her. Apparently, she was loved by everyone; well, not really, all the men loved her, but the wives were jealous. She was the only known lady to be allowed to attend a gentry board meeting, which was strictly a man's domain. Charles never mentioned her name, simply because she had outsmarted him and she was Irish. But secretly she admired her. One day she would take the girls to Ireland to meet their grandmother. All these thoughts and dreams dispersed when she heard her bedroom door opening. In came Charles, who had been drinking. Anne panicked; surely not tonight, so soon after losing his son, but Charles was on a mission, he wanted a replacement son, now! She could do nothing other than be the obedient wife. His bedside manner had not improved, it was still primitive. There was nothing in it for Anne. The duty was performed and he left.

The only time Anne saw Charles over the next few months was at night, when he came to her room in his mission to replace Albert. She longed to be with child, then he would stop coming. Sadly, Charles's feelings towards the girls had not changed; they were still just chattels. He had never asked to whom Lucy had gone, she was non-existent to him, as she was blamed for Albert's death. Her name was never spoken of in front of Charles. Anne and the girls were thankful that he had a business that took him off the estate each day. Only then could they discuss their dear sister Lucy. They loved getting letters from her and John and often discussed about going to Ireland one day to see them both. Their grandmother Mary seemed to be a kind, loving person and they would like to meet her, especially Anne as she wanted to thank her for taking in Lucy. Anne promised the girls she would take them to Ireland, but it would have to be without their father's knowledge, as he would forbid them this privilege.

The time had arrived that Anne had prayed for; she was with child. This meant no more visits from Charles. She hoped this would be her last child, then she could begin to live the life she dreamed of. The girls were getting older, so they would help her with the new baby. When Anne told them, they wished for another sister. But not Charles, this was his son and heir! He had already named him as Charles Albert Rothchild. "But Charles, we might have another daughter, we can't pick the gender of our child, we have to accept what we are given," Anne told him in a gentle manner. "I don't want another girl, this must be a son!" he roared. Once again, the subject of John was brought up. "But you are not without a son. Elizabeth gave you a son, he is a good lad. He is now a qualified engineer, you should be proud of him as I am." "I want an English son, not an Irish red-haired child," he stated. "But Charles, John is not a child, he is a man. Your mother and Connor are so proud of him, as you should be. One day you will regret you cast him aside as he may turn out to be your only son. Have you ever thought about that?" "He will never be a lord, we will keep having children until you produce me a son, Anne, that is your duty to me. Give me a son," he demanded. She could see this conversation was going in the direction it always headed. He was desperate for a son and heir, thus blinding his mind to any other outcome. She was very sad, but he was a lord, his arrogance came with the title, although his father Lord Albert was apparently a gentleman. Perhaps it came from his grandfather Lord Charles Rothchild. The aristocracy was known for their high-mindedness.

Anne had gone into labour through the night, but waited until the morning before asking Charles to take her to the hospital. She was anxious; what if she produced another daughter? How many more visits would she have to endure before she gave him a son? This thought was better erased from her mind until after the baby was born. Charles waited at the hospital, the hours ticked by and his agitation grew. Why hadn't Anne had the baby? He wanted to get back to the office. He summoned the nurse to see how long Anne was going to be. "Your wife is still in labour, she is having a difficult birth, this is not easy on her," she pointed out to Lord Charles. "Make sure nothing happens to my son," he told the nurse. She was upset; what about his wife? He never mentioned her. But she had seen this many times before with wealthy landowners; sons came before wives. Wives were easily replaced. Lord Charles took his leave from the hospital, he would come back later.

At the end of the day he closed his office and went back to the hospital, only to learn the baby had still not been born. Anne was very weak and the doctor was concerned.

If nothing happened soon, then the fate of the baby did not look good. He told Lord Charles this. "If it is a son, save him, I need a son," was the answer that came back. "But what of your wife? She is not well, we may have to make a decision either way," said the doctor. "We won't know the baby's gender before a decision has to be made." "Then save Anne, she can give me another son," and with this he left. This was not unusual behaviour, it was a fact of life.

Later that night Anne gave birth to a baby boy, but he only survived for an hour. She had gone through a hard labour and was exhausted, so she was not told, it could wait till the morning. When Charles came to see her the next morning, his heart was broken when he learned about the death of his son, that he had only survived for one hour. Anne was still sleeping so he went back to the estate. Once again, he was without an heir. But they would try again soon, he was adamant that it would happen next time! The girls were at school so he would wait until they came home to tell them. He couldn't go to work. He just wanted to mourn for his deceased son.

They would have a private burial; he didn't want to see the baby, it was hard enough knowing that he had lost him. After lunch he went back to the hospital to see Anne. She was upset at losing her baby; for all she had gone through, there was nothing to show for her pain. While Lord Charles was with his wife the doctor came in, as he wanted to speak with them together. "I'm very sad for your loss. I have more bad news to tell you, Anne. You cannot have any more children. This birth has caused damage that will not allow you to reproduce." "What do you mean?" asked an irate Charles. "There cannot be any more babies, Lord Charles." "But I need a son," he demanded. Anne was angry. "You already have a son, Charles, be thankful. Now leave," she told him. The doctor asked Lord Charles to leave as he had upset his wife. He was furious, no more children, what would he do now? What good was Anne if she couldn't give him a son?

After a week in hospital Anne was allowed home. She was still very weak and had to rest until she had fully recovered. The girls looked after their mother; they were sad about the baby, but they were happy to have her home. Their father wasn't of any help, as he was grieving and sulking, both at the same time. He showed no compassion for their mother and spent a lot of time at his law office. He distanced himself from his family. As Anne grew stronger and her grieving became less, she decided it was time to take the girls across to Ireland to meet their grandmother Mary. She was missing Lucy, she needed to see her. This could not be discussed in front of Charles.

Anne received an answer to her letter from Mary, stating they would be delighted for her and the girls to come and stay. The long school holidays were coming up, so this was when they would go. Anne spoke with Charles about taking the girls for a holiday and he was pleased about this. He would have the estate to himself, as he was still getting over the loss of his son. He had to make plans for the future. If Anne couldn't give him a son, he would have to think about a divorce, then take another wife, otherwise the Rothchild estate would cease to survive. This could not be allowed to happen, as it had been in the Rothchild family for generations. He had an obligation to fulfil, notwithstanding that he did already have a son, but not the English one he so desired.

13

A Tragedy at Sea

Anne and the girls were on the ferry on their way to Ireland. They were sitting out on a deck seat, talking about seeing Lucy again, they were so excited. Jane had never met John but she wrote him letters. They wondered what Grandmother Mary was like. Lucy loved her to bits and never wanted to leave, this was now her home. Anne was a little sad to hear this, as she was Lucy's mother, but it was Charles who had driven her away. There were no feelings in his heart for her. As she sat and thought about life with Charles, and what had unfolded in the past couple of months, she realised that she meant very little to him. Especially now that she couldn't provide him with a son. What of the future? she asked herself. The sea was quite choppy so Anne suggested they go indoors, but the girls were enjoying out on the deck. Her thoughts were broken by the sound of screaming. She looked around and the girls had been bumped off the seat and were lying on the deck. Anne ran to help them, when a warning came over the speaker. It was the captain telling all the people on the open deck to go immediately to an enclosed area. Anne would not leave her daughters so crawled along the deck to grab them, when a huge rogue wave swamped the deck and washed those passengers on deck overboard and out to sea.

John, Lucy and Grandmother Mary were waiting patiently at the docks for the ferry to arrive. It was late but the sea was rough, so perhaps it was delayed by the weather? They were excited as Lucy was going to see her mother and sisters again and Mary was going to meet her other grandchildren and their mother. But as time went by, there was no sighting of the ferry. People on the docks waiting for family and friends were becoming alarmed, but all they could do was wait. Two hours had passed when someone shouted that the ferry was coming. As it neared the land, it was only then they realised it was damaged and was limping into the port. Everyone waited with bated breath. As it got nearer, they could hear people wailing, and it was then they knew something bad had happened. Mary looked at John and prayed nothing had happened to their family.

As the ferry tied up at the wharf, the captain and crew came out on deck and yelled for any medical personnel to make their way to the gangway as they were needed on board immediately. No passengers were allowed off. Word had spread around the docks like wildfire so all doctors and nurses from any hospitals nearby were needed. None of the people waiting on the docks knew what fate was going to be bestowed upon them. Passengers were calling out to waiting friends that people had been washed overboard and many more were hurt. Thus the panic began! The captain came down the gangway and asked the people to stay calm, as there were people missing, they had been washed overboard, but until they did a head count and ticked the names off a clipboard, he was powerless to say much more. The crowds were yelling, demanding to know if their loved ones were safe.

Lucy looked to see if she could see her mother and sisters, but they were not there. "Grandmother, do you think they are safe?" she asked with tears in her eyes. Mary held her in her arms trying to comfort her. "Of course, my darling, they may be hurt, but they will be safe." Stretchers were being taken on board to bring the injured passengers to the waiting carriages, to take them to hospital. No-one was allowed near. The crew were ticking the injured people's names of the list before they were taken away. Once the injured were cleared, the able-bodied passengers were allowed to disembark and their names were ticked off. Darkness was now setting in and the police had just arrived to do a search of the ferry. Still there were no signs of Anne and the girls. Once all the passengers that had survived were accounted for, the captain now knew he had lost twenty-eight passengers. He gave the names to the police, whose job it was to inform the next of kin. Mary left Lucy with John and made her way to where the police were gathered. "Please tell me my family are safe," she asked. She gave the police the names and they were not ticked off. It was then Mary learnt the fate of her family. How was she going to tell Lucy her mother and sisters were gone? This was all the police could tell her at the moment, but an official list would be posted at the police station in the morning. Perhaps if she came back then there might be better news. "Is someone out looking for the missing persons?" she asked. The police said it was too risky for any search vessels to leave the port, but they would begin a search at first light. This did little to comfort Mary.

When realisation hit her, Mary remembered that Charles knew nothing of the family coming to Ireland. He would have no idea what had happened to them. But first and foremost came Lucy. As she made her way back to her grandchildren, she was grief-stricken. John knew as soon as he saw tears in Mary's eyes that something tragic had happened, not thinking for one moment that the whole family were gone. "Grandmother, where is everyone?" asked an anxious Lucy. Mary took her in her arms. "Lucy, I don't know what to say, but I will be truthful. Your mother and sisters are missing, my darling. I can't tell you any more, the police will speak with us tomorrow morning." "But they will be found, won't they, grandmother?" "We hope so, my darling," knowing full well that the outcome was going to be no different tomorrow to what it was today. By this time John had guessed what had happened, and he had to turn away so as to hide his tears from Lucy. He had to be brave for her. They huddled together along with other grief-stricken families; twenty-eight loved ones had perished. Mary organised for them to stay the night at a local inn. She would sleep with Lucy in her arms tonight, as tomorrow was going to be a terrible day for this little girl, as if she hadn't had enough sadness in her short life. Mary was heartbroken.

During the night Lucy woke. "Grandmother, my family will be safe, will we see them tomorrow?" she asked. "Sleep, my darling, we will wait and see what tomorrow brings." Mary couldn't go to sleep. What would the police tell them tomorrow that she didn't already know? But a little hope was better than no hope. Her two grandchildren were gone forever, and she didn't get the chance to meet them. And Anne, how she must have suffered, did she see her children washed overboard? It was unlikely anyone would survive a night in the stormy sea. How were they going to cope with such a tragedy?

When Mary woke in the morning, Lucy was already out of bed and dressed. "Hurry, grandmother, we have to get to the docks to find mother and my sisters, they will be waiting for us." Poor Mary, she just wanted to stay under the bedclothes and pretend none of this was happening. "You go and knock on John's door and I will get dressed," she told Lucy. She had to bathe her eyes, they were swollen from the tears she shed during the night. She knew what heartache they were about to face. The three of them made their way down to the police station, where a crowd had gathered. The captain and crew of the ferry were standing with the police. Everyone was there for the same reason, waiting to hear news of their loved ones. There was a police announcement. "Search vessels have been searching since first light, but no bodies have been recovered. The official list of the missing persons has been put on a notice board inside the police station. Only those who have lost loved ones are allowed to enter." "How did this happen?" yelled an angry voice from the crowd. The captain spoke: "The missing passengers were out on the deck when a rogue wave came and swept them overboard. I put out a call for the people to make it to an enclosed area, but it was too late, it all happened so quickly. I offer my condolences to those who have lost loved ones."

There was nothing more anyone could do, no amount of abuse was going to help the situation. The people were gone. On hearing this Lucy burst into tears. "Will mother and Sarah and Jane's name be on the list?" she asked. "Yes, my darling, they are missing at sea." "Does that mean they are gone forever?" she sobbed. "I will never see them again." Mary knelt down and took her granddaughter in her arms while she took all this in. She sobbed uncontrollably. "All our hearts are broken, Lucy. Your mother and sisters have perished together, their souls will never be parted, they will be together forever, always remember this, they will stay as a family." She hoped this would bring a little comfort to this devastated child. "What will father say?" she muttered among her sobs. "He will blame me like he did for Albert's accident. Am I bad, Grandmother Mary?" "No, my darling, you are not bad, you are a lovely little girl who has suffered so much misfortune, but none of this is your fault. You are our little angel sent to us, like John, from a father who is cruel and unkind.

"What do we do now, Grandmother Mary?" she asked. John, who was grieving quietly in the background, suggested they wait for all the search vessels to return, in case they had any further news. He would miss Anne and the girls. Anne had always been kind to him, she would stand up for him against his father. Now he had lost another crucial person in his life, as she was the only contact he and Lucy had to the estate. Now all connections were lost.

They made their way back to the inn to get something to eat, as breakfast had long gone. Lucy wouldn't eat, she was still in shock, she was never going to see her family ever again. Mary left her to grieve in her own way. John went and sat with his arms around her, as she was all he had left from his father's children, although they had different mothers. The ones they loved most were both gone. Thank God they had grandparents that took them in and cared for them. Mary watched them grieve together, she loved them both dearly. They were the only good that came from her son, and to think he disowned them, for no other reason than the colour of their hair.

They waited along with the other people until all the search vessels returned, but there were no bodies recovered. Mary decided they would go home, it would be better to get Lucy away from the wailing people, who like her had lost loved ones. Mary's family would be devastated as they were all looking forward to meeting Anne and the girls, instead they were returning empty-handed. But what of Charles? Perhaps it would be better for all if the police delivered the tragic news to him, then no-one would be in the firing line. If Lucy was to be blamed again for more bad news, it would have disastrous consequences, as she already thought she was a bad person. Besides, Charles didn't know she was living with Mary. If no bodies were recovered, there would be no funeral, so they wouldn't have to go back to the Rothchild estate. Mary would ask her church to hold a service for her family. Before they left town, Mary called at the police station and gave them Charles's details so they could contact him. This would leave the Irish clan out of the picture.

14

Charles's Empty Life

This morning Lord Charles woke with a hangover. The bottle of whisky he had consumed last night lay empty on the floor. With Anne and the girls away, he thought he would cherish having time on his own, but after several days he became lonely. Thus thoughts of George resurfaced. Why couldn't he let go of those memories? But they always came back when he felt alone. He dreamt of finding him again and bringing him back where he belonged. John was an adult now and living in Ireland, so perhaps George would come back, as there were no obstacles. He could be his personal butler again?

Charles's thoughts turned to Anne. How was he going to deal with this situation? He needed a son and she couldn't give him any more children. He would have to think about a divorce and taking a new wife, as time was marching on. He needed an heir. As he lay in bed thinking of these scenarios, he thought he heard someone calling his name. He jumped out of bed and drew the curtains, only to see a policeman standing on the lawn outside his window. Charles quickly dressed and made his way to where he was standing. "Can I help you?" "Are you Lord Charles Rothchild?" he asked. Charles nodded to him. "Could I please come in, as I have sad news for you?" Charles was worried; had something happened to George? He invited him in and they went into the drawing room, where he asked him to be seated. "What is wrong?" he asked. The policeman didn't know where to start. "Have you heard about the tragedy on the Irish Sea?" Charles had heard nothing. "There was a storm and twenty-eight passengers were swept overboard. Your wife and daughters are among the missing, presumed drowned. I'm very sorry to have to bring you this sad news," he said amid his tears. "What do you mean? My wife and daughters were on holiday, they never said anything about going to Ireland. Anne knew how I felt about the Irish," he said angrily. The policeman could not believe what he was hearing. Where was the grief? This was his wife and children who were missing. "I'm sorry, Lord Charles, this must be very distressing for you. The search vessels have called off any further searches as no bodies have been found. The Irish police said a lady and her two grandchildren were devastated when their loved ones didn't arrive. She was the one who gave us your details, her name was Mary O'Leary."

As soon as Lord Charles heard that name, he couldn't help but vent his anger. "What the hell was she doing there? She must have known Anne and the girls were coming. And who were the grandchildren?" He knew one would have been John, but the other, who was that? Why was his wife and children going to Ireland? Then it all became clear. Were they going to see Lucy? Was she also living with her grandmother? His only two surviving children were now in their grandmother's care. He had no-one, not even George. The policeman took his leave, as he thought this was all too much for Lord Charles, he wasn't thinking straight. Again, his anger surfaced, it was now the blame game. If Anne hadn't sent Lucy to Ireland to live with her grandmother, then this would not have happened, his family would not have been on that ferry. He wasn't for a moment caring about Lucy, she had caused enough strife. She was responsible for Albert's accident leading to his death. But to lose his wife and two children, he felt a little sad that they had met with such a tragic death.

Now the way was clear for Lord Charles to take a new wife. He didn't have to worry about getting a divorce. His heart was heavy, he was alone in his mansion on the Rothchild estate with no-one to share his wealth. When he told the cook and the gardener about the tragedy, they were devastated. The cook loved the girls. She knew what went on with Lord Charles; he was a selfish aristocrat, one who thought himself above the common working class. She thought he was being punished, but sadly it was the innocent people who suffered, not the one deserved of punishment. If she didn't need the money, she would have walked out on Lord Charles, but work wasn't easy to come by. Out of respect for Anne, Lord Charles arranged a service for his family.

Six months had gone by and Lord Charles was dating a young lady from a solicitor's office in town. It didn't take him long to get over Anne. She had told him not to come back to her room, so there was never going to be any more activity there, as she could give him no more children, on the doctor's orders. Not that he was a romantic or really interested in the opposite sex, but they had a duty to him, to give him the son he needed to carry on his name. This was the sole reason for him to take another wife. Her life would be no different to that of Elizabeth and Anne's. Catherine, like the wives before her, was impressed, and the thought of becoming Lady Rothchild and living on the beautiful estate impressed her. She felt sorry for Lord Charles, as he had lost his wife and children in a tragic accident. He needed someone to bring a little happiness into his life. She had accepted his proposal in marriage, although there was fifteen years' difference in their ages. She was infatuated with him and his wealth, so did not see this as a worry. She could have everything she desired and give up her boring job, sitting behind a desk in the solicitor's office, for a more privileged life. She was a young romantic at heart, so was carried along by her dreams. Lord Charles would be a seasoned lover; she had read about these older men, he could teach her many things! She was excited about this prospect of life with him. He would be her knight in shining armour.

They hadn't spent much courting time together as he was a busy man, but this would change? Catherine was sure he would be different when she came to live on the estate. She would keep him amused, she was young and full of vitality. She wasn't from Oxshott, nor the daughter of an estate owner, but Lord Charles was sure she was fertile and would give him children, especially a son.

The marriage took place just before the wheat harvest in Ireland and again it was looking like a bumper yield. Lord Charles's wealth was accumulating, but he could never match his mother's wealth, as she owned more farms than him. She was producing most of Ireland's wheat intake, and this was still a thorn in his side. He had no contact with John and Lucy; to him they didn't exist, not even his new wife knew of them. Catherine looked every bit the blushing bride and this was commented on by all the guests. She flitted from one guest to the next, full of excitement thinking of what lay ahead tonight. She controlled her alcohol intake, but noticed Lord Charles was over-indulging. She hoped this was not going to affect his bedroom performance.

After the last guest left, Catherine looked around for her husband, but he was not to be seen. She made her way to the drawing room but he wasn't there. Of course, he hadn't had a chance to lay down the house rules yet, they would have to wait to the morning. She searched the rooms and eventually found him sound asleep in what looked like his bed. She was disappointed, but she undressed and climbed in beside him, cuddling into him. There was no response so she drifted off to sleep. During the night Lord Charles stirred; he felt someone in his bed. His first thought was George was lying there with him and he began to cry, his lover had come back. Catherine was disturbed by her husband crying. "It's all right, Lord Charles, it's me, Catherine, your wife." With this he sat up in bed in shock. What was she doing in his bed? This was his and George's bed, no-one else shared his bed other than George. "Leave this minute, Catherine, this is my wing, you have your own. If I want you, I will visit you. Never come to my bed again." She was shocked, this was not what she expected on her wedding night. She climbed out of his bed and made her way to the other wing. She naturally thought they would sleep together so both needs could be met when each desired the other. But this was gentry style, this she would learn quickly, that the estate owners were the masters in their own home, so were entitled to their privacy. This life was all new to her. She climbed into bed bitterly disappointed; this was not what she imagined her wedding night to be. She cried herself to sleep.

The next morning at breakfast Lord Charles lay down the house rules. Catherine, as his wife, would call him Charles, but on official occasions she had to address him as Lord. His wing in the mansion was not to be entered; he would visit her when he wanted to perform his marital duties. Catherine was shocked. Since when did all this superiority begin? This was not the life she saw in her home. Was this what the upper class was all about? Perhaps she shouldn't have aimed so high in society. What happened to her dreams of the wonderful lovemaking they were going to be doing in their bed at nights? Were his feelings the only ones that mattered? What about hers? "Charles, this is not the life I want. Why can't I come to your bed when I am ready to make love?" she asked. "I will visit your room for one purpose only and that is for you to produce me children, a son first. I must have a son and heir to my estate. Now I have to go to work," and he left. Catherine's life and dreams collapsed right there and then. What did he mean? Did he want to perform his marital duties for the sole purpose of producing children? What about love? She was heartbroken. Like the wives before her, she was about to discover that being Lady Rothchild brought very little joy!

Charles came home for supper and poured himself a whisky before he sat down. The cook brought in the food and lay it on the dining table. "What did you do today,

Catherine?" he asked politely. She told him she spent most of the day in the rose gardens, as she loved roses. "Charles, when I want to go to town. Do I have my own carriage?" "Yes, I will show you how to set it up. You can use it whenever you want, your day is your own, that is until our son arrives, then you will be kept busy." During their supper Charles had three more whiskies. This made Catherine think she wouldn't see him tonight, but she felt she couldn't ask. As they said their goodnights it was just verbally, there was no show of affection. She felt let down once again.

She had saved and bought lovely silk nightdresses to wear to bed, so as to please her husband. As she climbed into bed, she felt disappointed. She lay there thinking of all the wonderful thoughts that filled her mind. Then she heard the door opening, and her sadness was replaced by excitement; he was coming to her. He got into bed beside her, climbed on top of her, and within minutes it was all over and he was on his way out the door. Was that all he had to offer her? What did she feel? Nothing but hurt to herself and hurt to her body. He was not at all gentle, he was rough and clumsy. Was this what she had to endure each time he visited her? Where were his feelings? They certainly weren't there tonight; this was just a chore to him. Little did Catherine know of his secret life. If she did, she would know he only had feelings for one person, that being George. The sole purpose of a wife was to bear him children. He would service her and by doing this, he expected results. It was not a pleasurable pastime for Charles.

The next morning Catherine didn't come to breakfast; her eyes were swollen as she had cried most of the night. Was this what she was going to be confronted with whenever he came to her room? When she wandered into the dining room later, the cook asked her if she could get her something to eat. She could see she had been crying. "What is wrong, Lady Catherine?" she asked. Catherine told her she was upset with Charles. In her innocence she confided in the staff. She was young and full of expectations, but so far none of these had been met.

"Neither of Lord Charles wives were happy souls, he was very demanding of them to produce him with a son. His first wife, Elizabeth, gave him a son, but he was born with the 'Irish curse', so he disowned him," she told Catherine. "What is the 'Irish curse'? Where is he, did he perish with the family?" she asked. "The 'Irish curse' is the red Irish hair, and he is living with his Irish grandmother in Ireland, as is his daughter Lucy." "But I though he had lost all his children. Who is Lucy?" Catherine enquired. "Lucy is a daughter to his second wife, Anne, but Lord Charles banished her after Albert was hurt." Then she went on to tell her about Lucy's accident and how she was scarred because of Lord Charles's neglect of his daughters. "The children born with the Irish hair have been shunned by their father, yet he is the one with the Irish blood in his veins. His mother, Mary, was Irish and quite an astute lady, by what I have heard, not that you will hear her name mentioned on this estate," said the cook. Catherine was bewildered with all this information, now realising that she had entered this relationship knowing very little about Charles. So, he already had two children, whom he never talked about. What was going to happen if she produced children with the 'Irish curse'? She would talk to Charles tonight.

Catherine sat and waited, but Charles never arrived home for his supper, so she ate on her own. She opened a bottle of wine to help drown her sorrows and by the end of supper the bottle was empty and her sorrows had disappeared. Her head was a little woozy so she retired to her room. She lay on her bed fully clothed and fell asleep. She didn't hear Charles entering her room, and awoke when she felt her clothes being ripped from her body. She tried to sit up, but he was in a rage. "When I come to your room, I expect you to be ready for me, I don't expect to have to remove your clothes!" he yelled at her. "But Charles, we should want to undress and touch each other." Never had either of his other two wives spoke to him like this, but then Catherine was younger. "I am serving you and it is your duty to repay me with a son!" he shouted. "I am not an animal, that's what they do, serve. I want to be loved," Catherine told him. With this he slapped her face. "You will do what I ask, you are here to give me a son, that is why I come to your room, for nothing else." With this he performed his duty and left. She now faced the truth: he didn't love her, she was there for the sole purpose of providing him with a son. All she was was a mere chattel, one to be used for a specific purpose.

This morning Catherine asked the gardener to set up the horse and carriage as she was going into town to meet a friend. She felt she had to confide in someone close to her. Being younger and from an ordinary background, it was not uncommon to talk about personal matters. The wives of the gentry did not discuss these things, nothing went outside the marriage; they accepted their fate. But for Catherine life was different; the stuffy aristocrat life was not what she envisaged her life to be. All she wanted was a loving husband, but this is not what she got. Her dreams of everything being wonderful upon becoming Lady Rothchild had all but vanished in a very short period of time. It was too late to change; she was powerless, her path had been made, now she must follow it. The only positive thing about her life was the luxury she lived in and the beautiful gardens that surrounded the estate. Having confided in her friend, she felt a little better, but nothing had changed. All her friend could do was lend a friendly ear and wish her well. As she drove home, she thought about Charles's two children. Perhaps she could speak to him about them tonight.

At supper Charles talked about his wheat yield in Ireland. This was the first time he had talked business with her. "Do you ever go to Ireland, Charles?" she asked him. "Never, nor will I ever. I hate the Irish." "But you have two children living in Ireland. Don't you want to visit them?" she asked. "They mean nothing to me, they were born with the 'Irish curse'." "What do you mean, the 'Irish curse'?" "They have the red Irish hair," he answered. "Where did that come from?" she enquired, knowing the story, but trying to make him admit it came from him. "All I will say is I want an English son. Don't give me a son with red hair!" "But Charles, if there is Irish blood somewhere, you have got to expect this to happen. If it is in the bloodline you cannot escape it," Catherine pointed out to him. This, he did not want to hear. He stormed out of the room; he would not have any of his shortcomings discussed with his wife. Catherine didn't see him for the rest of the night.

Six months had passed and Catherine was plagued with morning sickness. Charles had fulfilled his marital duties so he was relieved of his nightly visits. Catherine was also relieved; now she would not have to put up with his erratic behaviour in her bedroom. But she was suffering, pregnancy was not agreeing with her. She could hardly get out of bed in the mornings, only when she needed to be sick. She hoped this wasn't going to last for long. The doctor was concerned; if this didn't stop soon, she would have to be admitted to hospital. But as time went by the sickness left her and she started to feel normal again, apart from her expanding belly. Several times she had asked Charles to touch her and feel the baby, but he refused. He was only interested in the real thing, none of this before-the-event stuff. She had heard so many times that he wanted an English son, so one day she answered him back. "Charles, I can only give you what you give me, so if you don't get your son, it is not of my doing." This was the last time he mentioned this subject, as the truth hurt. For Catherine, the time seemed to stand still, as she still had another six weeks to go.

Today she had to help the cook prepare hors d'oeuvres, as there was a gentry board meeting being held on the estate. She watched as they pulled up in their flash carriages and went into the boardroom. She had to serve the men food in the drawing room following the meeting. She was looking quite radiant; being with child had certainly brought out the colour in her cheeks, not that Charles noticed. But during the after-meeting gathering, one person did notice how radiant Catherine looked; he even mentioned this to her personally, but not within earshot of anyone else. She blushed, as these were the first kind words spoken to her since her marriage. Suddenly she felt her self-worth creeping back into her life. Who was this gentleman? She could not ask Charles, he would be angry with her. Never mind, she would probably never see him again.

Catherine was in labour. It all happened quickly, so Charles had to rush her to the hospital. Soon he would have his son! He sat and waited, he heard screams. Was that his wife? Why did she have to be so vocal? This went on for an hour. He sat and blocked his ears, surely this was uncalled for, he thought to himself. Then there was silence and within minutes, a nurse came through to tell Lord Charles he had a little girl. Not the news he wanted to hear. "Your baby is healthy and has beautiful red hair." This only added fuel to the fire; the 'Irish curse' had struck again. Then he remembered Catherine's words: 'I can only give you what you give me'. As much as he didn't want to admit this was the truth, he was angry with her; she didn't deliver what he asked for. "Would you like to see your baby?" the nurse asked. "No, I will come back later," and he left. The nurse knew Lord Charles, and this was not unusual behaviour from him. When Catherine saw her baby, immediately her thoughts were of the 'Irish curse', but she would still love her. Secretly she was happy, as she wanted a little daughter with the Irish hair, just to annoy Charles.

This would teach him that one just had to take what one was given and be thankful, as long as they were healthy. But with this came consequences; he would be visiting her again at night until he got his son. That night when Charles came to visit Catherine at the hospital, she said to him, "Isn't she lovely, Charles? I'm so happy we have a beautiful little girl." "I'm not happy, Catherine, I wanted a son," he answered, but he failed to mention the red hair. He remembered her words. The next day she had a visitor; it was the young gentleman who had made her blush at the boardroom after-gathering. "Hello, Catherine, how are you feeling today? I am Dr Michael, I'm from the neighbouring estate." Catherine blushed, she was shocked to know he was a doctor. She told him she was fine. "You look well, you have recovered quickly after giving birth, keep up the good work," he said with a smile as he walked away. Her eyes followed him as he left the room. Even after having just given birth, she felt her heart give a little flutter; this was something she had never experienced before.

Each day Catherine looked forward to the young doctor visiting the patients in hospital. He would stop at her bed and chat with her. He was a breath of fresh air. "I haven't seen Lord Charles here very often?" he asked. "No, he is disappointed that I gave him a daughter, especially with the 'Irish curse'," answered Catherine. "What do you by the 'Irish curse'?" "The red Irish hair, he hates it. He demanded an English son but I produced him an Irish daughter," she said between her tears. "But she is beautiful, any man would be proud of her." "Not my husband," she sobbed. Michael sat on her bed and took her hand. "If this was my daughter, I would be so happy." Catherine had never heard such kind words. "Oh Michael, if only you knew," she said. He could sense this was a cry for help. "You are leaving to go home tomorrow. Make an appointment to come and see me when you feel well enough," he told her. She smiled through her tears. "Yes, I will, thank you."

It had been two months since Catherine came home to the estate. She loved her little daughter, whom she named Alice. Charles wasn't interested in girls' names, he barely noticed her as he was still disappointed that he didn't have a son. He had hinted on several occasions that he was keen to try for a son, but Catherine told him it was too soon, she was not ready. This only added to his petulant behaviour. Every day she thought of Michael; he was so kind and these thoughts made her happy. One day soon she would take up his offer and visit him.

Several weeks later Catherine had a visit from Charles; he was ready to do his duty. She felt cold, there was nothing about him that made her feel she could accept him. "No, Charles, I'm still breastfeeding Alice, I can't conceive while I am feeding so I don't want you to visit me." With this he left. She felt there was something strange about him, he had no love in his body, it was used as a tool to suit a purpose. One day while he was at work, she made her way to his room. She knew it was out of bounds to her, but why? She let herself in and walked around. It was the first time back since her wedding night, when she came to this very room and was told to leave. She looked around and felt a cold chill creep down her spine. Then she spied a key sitting on the dresser, so she picked it up. It fitted the top drawer, so she opened it. On the top sat a letter addressed to 'Lord Charles'. She wondered if she should read it, but perhaps she could learn something about him that she didn't know.

She picked it up and started reading: 'Lord Charles, these are my final words to you. We will never meet again. Since the day Elizabeth entered our room and found us in bed together, I can't help but think we both contributed to her death ...' It was George's final letter to Charles. Catherine was shocked and as she reached the end, the tears flowed uncontrollably and she stood shaking. What sort of man had she married? She had to get out of his room, she felt as though she was choking, as if there was no air left for her to breathe. She quickly folded the letter and put it back into the envelope, then locked the drawer and left. Now she knew why Charles acted the way he did; he preferred males to females. She was just a means to give him children. She felt sick, and ran to her room where she lay on the bed and howled like a lost child. What sort of man was she living with? Just the thought of him made her cringe. How were there going to be any more children?

Catherine was sitting in the doctor's waiting room. She was so distraught, she needed help. She had Alice with her, as Charles was at work. "Come in, Catherine, what can I do for you?" he asked her politely. She didn't know where to start, she couldn't tell him what she had uncovered about Charles. "Something has happened, I can no longer bear my husband near me. Can you give me something, as he wants a son?" she sobbed. "But it is too soon for him to make demands on you. Does he not realise this?" He took her hand and squeezed it, and suddenly a warmth came over her. Then he took Alice from her and bounced her on his knee. "What a beautiful little girl. What is her name?" he asked. "I called her Alice, I think it suits her." "It certainly does, you should be very proud." As he stood up and went to give Alice back to Catherine, his body brushed against hers, sending a tingle through her. "We are neighbours. Call in one day when you are passing, I would like that. Bring Alice with you," he told her. "Now I will give you something that will help you. Tell Lord Charles he must be patient, these things cannot be rushed." Catherine stood up and thanked him, then she did something that was so out of character for her. She leaned over and kissed him on his cheek. "Don't forget to call in, I will look forward to your visit," he told her as she was about to leave his room. Then she realised what she had done. "I'm sorry, please forgive me?" she said. "I'm not," came back his answer. She was so embarrassed, fancy being so forward, she didn't know what came over her. Was it because he was so kind to her and he liked her baby? But she knew the answer, it went deeper than that; he had stirred feelings in her body, feelings she had never felt before.

One day as Catherine was on her way to town, she saw Dr Michael at his gate fixing a fence. He waved for her to stop. "Hi, Catherine, come and have a cup of tea with me. I've just finished here and deserve a drink, but not on my own. Will you join me?" With this he climbed up and sat next to her as she drove down his driveway. "Where's Alice?" he asked. "She is in the carriage sleeping," she answered. She felt nervous, her heart was racing, beside her was the man of her dreams, if only he knew, she thought. They pulled up at the front entrance. The estate was not as grand as the Rothchild estate but it had a friendly feel about it. Michael jumped down and help Catherine alight, then he opened the carriage door and lifted out the basket with Alice in; she was still sound asleep. "How is my little one today?" he asked. Just hearing him talk about Alice with such love in his voice melted her heart. "Come on in. My housekeeper is away today, so please excuse the dishes," he apologised. "This is lovely, Michael, it has a warm lived-in feeling. Do you live here on your own?" "Yes, my parents passed away last year so the estate was left to me. I studied to be a doctor, so now I am an estate owner, with a medical doctorate," he said with a laugh. Catherine laughed with him; it was so nice to be able to share a happy moment with someone. She went to the sink to wash the dishes on the bench. "No, you are my guest. Sit down while I make the tea," he instructed her.

They talked nonstop over their cups of tea, both laughing and enjoying each other's company. Michael told Catherine about his life and she shared a little of hers with him. He could see she wasn't in a happy marriage, but why, he would give anything to have her as his wife. She was young and pretty but above all she was a doting mother. Catherine insisted on helping with the washing up, so she rolled up her sleeves and started to wash the dishes, while Michael grabbed the tea towel. She couldn't resist splashing a little water on his face and he retaliated, splashing her back. Then the laughter started. He wiped her face with the tea towel, in return she dried him and before either knew, they were locked in each other's arms. A fiery passion had overtaken them both. Catherine wanted him, she was ready. "Please love me, Michael?" she asked him. He picked her up and carried her through to his bedroom, then lay her on his bed. "Are you sure you want this to happen?" he asked her. "I want you to take me, to make love to me," she whispered. As he undressed her, his hands caressed her body touching all the appropriate places, places she never knew were so tender and tingly. His hands moved skilfully over her, she was writhing around on the bed, loving every minute, every touch. This was so satisfying, why had she not experienced this before? These feelings were what she dreamed of, but they had never come to fruition, until now. Her body felt alive with passion, she wanted him to take her so she could be part of him, so begged him to come to her. He was gentle in his loving, making her cry out in sheer delight. What was happening? She had never felt these feelings ever? They both lay exhausted in each other's arms, until they heard a whimper from the dining room. Alice had stirred. "That was beautiful, Michael, I feel so complete," she told him. "That makes two of us, my darling."

Six months had passed and Catherine was a different person. She was happy now that she had found love. She and Michael were secret lovers. She had managed to keep putting Charles off by telling him she was still breastfeeding, but in fact she had stopped two months ago. Then one morning she woke feeling sick. This carried on for several weeks until she realised she was with child. What would she do? Would she tell Michael? On her next visit to his estate he noticed her cheeks were very flushed. "Catherine, is something wrong? You look flushed." She told him she was with child. "Am I the baby's father?" "Yes, Michael, I haven't slept with Charles since Alice was born. What am I going to do?" "Will you leave him for me?" he asked. "I can't, he will take Alice from me. I couldn't bear to part with her, she is only a baby. If I didn't have Alice I would walk out tomorrow," she told him. They talked it over and agreed to leave things the way they were for the time being. "I will have to let Charles visit me, to let him think the baby is his until we work things out," she said with tears in her eyes. She hated this thought, now that she knew he preferred men; it nearly made her sick thinking about it, but she had no other choice!

Charles had noticed that Catherine seemed happy lately, perhaps she was ready to be served? That night he made his way to her room. She heard the door open, she wanted to tell him to go away, but she knew what she had to do. It would only be a quick visit so she would close her eyes and think of Michael. No, that would be an insult, she couldn't tarnish his image, she loved him too much. She would just have to lie there and be prepared for whatever was going to happen. As usual she could smell alcohol on him, so turned her face away; she couldn't bear the sight of him so close to her. He did his deed in his usual rough manner, but instead of leaving, he lay in her bed and drifted off to sleep. When his snoring started, Catherine left her bed and went to a spare room. She refused to share a bed with him for a minute longer than was necessary. When he woke in the morning, he reached over for Catherine, as he wanted to do his deed again. He needed a son as soon as possible, but the bed was empty. He went in search of her, but she was up and dressed. He could see her in the garden smelling the roses. She did look happy!

After two more visits from Charles, she told him not to come back, as she was sure she was with child. This made him happy, a son at last. He knew she would give him plenty of children as she was young and fertile. He couldn't get over how happy she seemed. She would often take the carriage and she and Alice would go places. Whatever she was doing seemed to make her smile all the time; she was pleasant to come home to. He had never heard her singing before, but now it was something she did most of the time. She spent a lot of time in the rose garden among the roses; this was where she felt the air was breathable, as wonderful memories flooded her mind. She loved Michael's home, it had a warmth about it, something the Rothchild estate did not have. It wasn't as glamorous, but by now, Catherine had realised that wealth didn't amount to anything, it was only a figure of speech, but happiness spoke in volumes! She couldn't wait till she and Alice visited Michael; there Alice was loved and cuddled as if she was his child. He loved her Irish hair, he said it shone like gold in the sunlight.

The months went by and Catherine's belly was very large. She was struggling at the end of her pregnancy. The only thing that kept her happy was knowing it was Michael's baby; she couldn't wait to see what it looked like. She was overdue a week but didn't tell Charles as this would have him wondering! Then one morning it all happened. She went into labour and within six hours the baby was born, then minutes later the second baby arrived. She had given birth to twin boys. When told, Charles was over the moon; he now had not one but two sons. He asked the nurse to take him to the nursery to see his sons. There lay two dark-haired little babies, side by side. Thank goodness the 'Irish curse' had gone at last. This time he couldn't wait to see Catherine but she refused to see him. The nurse told him this was probably due to her being tired, and she just wanted to sleep. Michael was the only person she wanted to share this wonderful moment with; she had given him two healthy sons. He was thrilled as now he had children of his own. He would keep her in hospital until he thought she could manage at home; this would give him a chance to spend the next few days holding and cuddling his babies. She hated the thought of seeing Charles. He would be gloating about his English babies, but they weren't his.

The next day Charles came to visit Catherine and was surprised to see a lovely bunch of flowers on her side dresser. "Where did they come from?" he asked. "I thought you must have brought them," she said, knowing full well Michael had given them to her. This went right past Charles! The subject was dropped. He wanted to discuss names for the babies. "We will have family names for my sons," he told her. "No, Charles, you can name one and I will name the other," she told him sternly. "What do you mean, Catherine, they are my sons, they will have family names. I am calling them Charles and Albert Rothchild, this I have decided." "No, I am naming one Michael John and you can name the other Charles Albert." He left it at that, he wasn't going to argue with her, but this was not going to be a happening thing. No way. Where did the name Michael come from anyway?

Charles couldn't wait for Catherine to bring his sons home, but her stay in hospital was longer than he had hoped. She seemed okay to him. Why wasn't she back at the estate where his sons belonged? He spoke with Dr Michael demanding that she be allowed out, he needed her at home. "You must realise, Lord Charles, Catherine will be feeding two babies plus she will have Alice to care for. She must be able to cope. When we think she is well enough to go home, we will let you know." He wanted to make sure Catherine would be able to look after his babies and Alice; it was a big ask. Catherine promised Michael she would bring the babies and Alice to see him as often as possible, but it might not be for a couple of weeks after she got home. "I will make an excuse to come and see you and my sons after a week," he told her. She didn't know how she would react when she saw Charles cuddling the babies, she didn't even want him to touch them, now that she knew what he was. But this could not be revealed, as it wouldn't look good for her, society would shun them both. The night before she was due to leave, Michael was on call at the hospital, so it gave him time to spend with his babies. He was going to miss them, but he knew Catherine would see no harm came to them, she was a good mother.

Catherine was holding one baby and Michael was holding the other when Charles pulled up to take them home. He climbed down from the carriage and rushed at Michael to take his son from him; his job as the doctor was finished. Catherine was not happy to be going home, although she missed Alice; the cook had stayed on to look after her while Catherine gave birth. At least she knew Charles would not be coming to visit her at nights, thank

God! He had his two sons, and as it held no pleasure for him to do so, that duty was over. She would have Michael, who was loving and tender with her. They shared laughter and other pleasures that made her feel like a woman again, not just a chattel to be used!

Of course, the babies' names had to be sorted and this was an ongoing battle. But Catherine stood her ground, she would not give in to Charles, and he was just as stubborn. His anger was demonstrated one night when he hit her, leaving her with a black eye, but this didn't make her buckle under pressure; for once she was going to have her way. She knew he would favour one child over the other because of the name, but she wouldn't let this worry her, as she didn't know how long she would stay with him. Charles sulked for days because he didn't get his own way. Eventually the twins were named Albert Charles and Michael John Rothchild.

15

Drama at the Estate

Two years had passed and the twins were growing into healthy young boys. Alice loved her brothers. They visited Uncle Michael often, but Alice wasn't allowed to tell her father, as Daddy would be angry; this was their secret. The twins were too young to understand but it wouldn't be long before Catherine would have to rethink her situation. Then the unthinkable happened, she was with child again. This could not be Charles's baby as he had not visited her since the twins were born. He had his family. She asked him if he wanted another baby but he did not, so refused to visit her. Of course, Michael was happy, as he hoped Catherine would leave Lord Charles and come to live on his estate with his sons and Alice. As the weeks passed Charles noticed something was different with Catherine. She still seemed happy but things were getting on top of her, she was finding it hard to cope. "I will hire a nanny to look after the children," he told her. "No, Charles, I don't want anyone to look after my children, they are my responsibility. I'm not well at the moment but I will get better soon." She was hoping the morning sickness would pass, but it was persistent. One morning Charles saw her rushing off to the bathroom, so he followed her and heard her vomiting. Then he knew she wasn't well. "Go to the doctor, Catherine, something is wrong," he told her. But she refused. How much longer could she keep this from Charles? It was all about to come out in the open.

Charles noticed Catherine was putting on weight. What was wrong? he wondered. As the weeks progressed, he noticed the weight was around her middle area. The time had come! "Catherine, what is wrong?" "I am with child," she told him. He stood there shocked. But how? He hadn't visited her since the twins were born. "No, that can't be true?" he questioned. "Yes, Charles, I am with child. I have taken a lover, how do you think I could live without love? You never gave it to me, you used me as a chattel, not as a lover. I am a woman, I need to be loved, not used. But another man did, he showed me what love was, it was beautiful. Nothing you did with me could be described in this way." "Who is this man? I will kill him!" shouted Charles. "No, you brought this on yourself. Wealthy you might be, but as a lover you are useless, less than a man, more like a beast the way you treat a woman. I am going to leave you, I can't stomach you a minute longer." "Catherine, how can you say that? I gave you a daughter and two sons, was that not enough?" he asked. "No, Charles, you did give me Alice, but not the boys," she told him. "What do you mean?" "The twins belong to my lover, you have no sons apart from John. Michael and Albert are not your sons," she said. "That is a lie, Catherine, they are my sons. I served you." "Yes, you served me, what a shocking word to use. I'm not an animal, I need more than to be served, but I was nearly three months with child when you visited me," she told him. Charles was devastated. Was this the truth? He was so angry he lunged at Catherine, he wanted to hurt her. "You can do what you like to me, Charles, but the twins' father will come after you. I know your dirty little secret. I know what George was to you, your lover. I read his letter in your drawer and was disgusted when I found out. To think you preferred males over females made me sick. You used your wives as chattels, but not any more, Charles. I will expose you if you don't let go of the twins, Alice and myself. We want no part of you. The decision is yours! Set the children and me free and I will stay silent about your secret life."

Charles's world had come tumbling down. He was a lord and owned the Rothchild estate, but that was all. Catherine had gone with the children, he didn't know where. His secret life had to remain a secret, he couldn't afford for it to be exposed. It would affect his standing among the gentry, so it had to remain just that ... a secret, but at such a cost! When Charles learned that his neighbour Dr Michael was Catherine's lover, he was devastated, but he could do nothing. Catherine, like his mother, Mary, had beat him at his own game.

Charles's health had taken a turn for the worst. The heartbreak he had suffered affected him and took him to a new low. He became depressed and drank excessively. He had no-one. All his energy to produce a son had come to nothing. He had fathered six children, John, Sarah, Lucy,

Jane, Albert and Alice, but only three of these children were still living. Two had been disowned, and of these, one was his only surviving son, John. He had to try to find George, he needed him, but he didn't know where to start. The only person that would know would be John, but he had had no contact with him in years; he was living in Ireland. Lord Charles remembered that George had looked after John when he went to boarding school, perhaps he still lived in that area. He would catch a train to Wakefield and begin his search. George was all he had left!

After spending two days in Wakefield his search for George had yielded nothing. He decided to go the Boys Grammar School where John was a boarder, perhaps they might have an address for George. He hired a carriage to take him out to the school. They stopped at the school gate and Charles alighted. He asked the driver to wait for him as he wouldn't be long. He walked towards the building, then someone caught his eye and he stopped. There was George working in the school gardens; this was how he had met him in the first place, at his college where he was the gardener. His heart beat faster, he had found him at last! He had aged well, far better than Lord Charles, but he had always been a fit young man. The closer he got, the more excited he became. "Hello, George," he called out. George knew that voice and spun around, only to be faced by Lord Charles. He had aged, he looked pale and gaunt. He was shocked, as he never thought he would see him again. His life had turned out happy since John went to Ireland, it left him free to find a new partner and they were still together. What was Lord Charles doing here? They stared at each other, neither knowing what to say.

Charles broke the silence. "Is this where you worked when John was here?" "Yes, I was his mentor, he depended on me and I was here for him. He has done well for himself, hasn't he?" asked George, knowing that they were still estranged. "I don't know, I have no contact with him," replied Lord Charles. "Connor has taken him in partnership with him in his engineering business. He has met a lovely Irish lass and they are to be married soon. I am invited to the wedding, I will be there," George let him know. Lord Charles was shocked; all this was happening and he knew nothing, but this was his son, why didn't he know any of this? "George, I need you back in my life, I am lonely," he pleaded. He told George where his life was at. "Sorry, Lord Charles, I have a partner whom I have been with for a long time, we are very happy. I wrote in my letter to you that one day you would regret the way you treated those close to you, especially your family, and now you are paying the price. It is probably too late for you to make amends. Your son John is the nicest young man I have ever known, I am so proud of him; we still write to each other. Remember all the letters he wrote to you and you didn't have the decency to answer? What sort of father would do that? You have lost the one closest to your heart, your son, Lord Charles. I will never come back to you, those years of my life I feel were wasted, to see such cruelty to family members, especially your and Elizabeth's son. It hurt me so much, I had to get away from the Rothchild estate and you."

Tears filled Lord Charles's eyes; apart from Catherine and his mother, no-one had talked to him in this way. "Please leave, Lord Charles, you have broken many hearts; not mine, but family members'. Now is your time to do penance and put right all those lives you have ruined. Such tragedies have befallen you, but sadly the innocent ones have gone. Start with your mother and your son;

if you can't find forgiveness in your heart you will die a lonely old man." After saying this, George turned his back and walked away. Lord Charles was devastated, not even the love of his life wanted him any more. The tears flowed as he walked towards the gates where the carriage was waiting. "Are you all right, sir?" asked the driver. He was so grief-stricken, he just nodded his head. Where to from here?

Being back home on the estate didn't make Charles happy any more. He had all the wealth but not a soul to share it with. Sometimes he would see Catherine and the children in town; it broke his heart, he wanted to approach them but he knew the consequences. At night he would take the top off a bottle of whisky and drink until he fell asleep. In the morning the self-pity would start. One day, the staff at his law office told him to take an extended holiday, as they had watched him slowly destroying himself.

But where would he go? Then George's words came flooding back to him: 'Start with your mother and your son'. He didn't want to end up a lonely old man, he needed someone, he had everything material, but no-one he felt close to. George was never going to come back. All those years that had passed, he held on to hope that he would return to him, but now those thoughts were futile. He was hurting deep down, he would never take another wife because of what Catherine had told him about himself, that he used women and, in the end, they were disgusted with him. Perhaps he should go to Ireland. No, he hated the Irish and Ireland, but why? he asked himself. He couldn't find a reason why he shouldn't go.

16

Was Penance About to Happen?

Lord Charles sat on the deck of the ferry as it was crossing the Irish Sea; he put his head in his hands and cried. This was the first time he thought of Anne and his daughters Sarah and Jane in a long time. This was where their lives had tragically ended. He had been too consumed in his own selfish life, now just to sit and reflect brought feelings to him that he didn't know he had. As he cried, he could see them before him. Why did he not have these feelings when they were alive? Now it was too late, they were gone. What about Lucy? How did she feel when she was told her mother and sisters were gone? She had no-one except her Irish family; he had cast her aside, for what? As he thought back over his life, he felt ashamed, he had hurt so many people, he had turned them against him. Could he change, could he make amends and turn things around?

Once upon a time he did love his mother, Mary. She was beautiful, his father adored her, and all he did was cause his family heartache. For the first time since they had left the estate, he thought of his half sister and brothers. He had turned them against him because of his spoilt and arrogant ways. Then there was Joseph, his brother, who he shot so he could be the eldest and inherit the peerage to become a lord. He cringed when he thought of all the shame he had brought on himself. None of them cared about him and now he understood why. And his son John; George was so proud of him. Why George? It should have been him that was proud. Why wasn't he? Because he had disowned him from a little child, simply because he had the red Irish hair. The 'Irish curse', where did that come from? Himself, of course. Fancy telling a child that they were cursed. He was disgusted with himself. What was happening, why was he cross-examining himself, was this a new beginning? Was he starting his penance?

On his arrival, he asked at the wharf where he could get somewhere to stay. The people were polite and helpful, someone even walked with him to point out where the inn was situated. He made his way along the street and entered the inn. He decided to spend one night in Cork before taking a carriage to Dunmanway tomorrow. He still had so much to think about. The inn staff were very pleasant. What happened to the Irish people he thought he hated? He settled into his room and lay on the bed to rest. So much was running through his mind, his brain closed down and he drifted off to sleep. When he woke in the morning, he realised this was the first time in months that he had not gone to bed with a bottle of whisky. He was able to sleep without it! He felt happy, his head was clear, so he decided to have some breakfast. He ate a hearty meal of bacon and eggs with freshly baked bread. Even the food tasted good. Why was everything so different? he asked himself. Was it the Irish air, or was his penance beginning? Perhaps it was forgiveness finding its way into his body. He was even looking forward to his carriage ride to Dunmanway today.

As they left the city of Cork and entered into the countryside, it was the start of the wheat country. The crops were turning gold, it was a glorious sight. Some of these farms he owned, which ones, he didn't know. The colour gold brought a rare smile to his face, this was the land that afforded his luxury lifestyle. These people worked to provide him with all the material things he desired, but little else! As they travelled close to some of the farmhouses, he felt sad; some were rundown, others were falling down. He asked the carriage driver to stop. "Look at those houses. Is that what the families live in, who work the farms?" he asked. "Yes, sir, that is the English gentry for you, they care little for the tenant farmers who work their lands. All this land was once owned by our people, but it was taken from them by the then King of England and given to his own knights and helpers. Now the Irish are virtually slaves on their own land. We are a humble race of people, and proud of our Irish heritage," he explained. "Drive on," said Lord Charles with a wave of his hand. He was horrified, tears came to his eyes. No wonder his mother stood up for her people against the gentry. She tried to protect them, to make a better life for the tenant farmers. They lived in hovels and owned nothing. What of the children? Were they fed, how did they keep warm in homes without glass in the windows? All his years on the estate, he never gave a thought to the conditions that the tenant farmers worked under. Now that he saw it first-hand, it was appalling. The land was fertile and rich, but living conditions were shocking. As they reached Dunmanway he asked the driver to drop him off at an inn in the town. This was his first visit since all those years ago when they came and buried Joseph at the church here. He was just a young boy, so had no memories of Ireland, just that he thought he hated it.

After settling in under the name of Charles Rothchild, he asked where the church was, as he wanted to visit his brother's grave. On the way he bought some flowers, first time ever, to lay by the headstone. When he reached the church, he walked around the back to the graveyard. He searched for Joseph Rothchild's headstone, but he could not find it. He knew it was beside his grandfather James Nyhan though. But all that was there was a beautiful headstone with Joseph O'Leary inscribed on it. He stopped to read it and yes, it was his brother. But why O'Leary, not Rothchild? He laid the flowers and went and sat on a seat near the grave. Why would he be buried under that name? It was the surname of his half sister and brothers, who were younger than him, but Joseph was the eldest of the children. Did his mother have Joseph before she met his father, was he only his half-brother? If this were true, then he was never in line to inherit the title of Lord. Had he died in vain? Was this a needless death that he had caused because of his obsession to become a lord? He cried uncontrollably. Here before him was the reminder of another tragedy that had unfolded, all because of him. He felt old and tired; he would be only forty-nine next birthday.

Several hours had passed. He must had nodded off, as he was disturbed by a young man walking past him. He watched as he placed flowers on James Nyhan's headstone. That was Charles's grandfather, his mother Mary's father. He wondered who the young gentleman was, so he asked him. "I'm Brendon Carey, this is my wife's grandfather, that is her brother Joseph buried next door," he said. Lord Charles hid his head in shame. This was his sister Rose's husband, the one he had been so horrible to. He had called him a nobody, he even tried to throw him off his farm. The shame he had brought on himself was almost unbearable, but now he was coming to terms with what a wicked person he had been. "Where are you from?" the young man asked. "Oh, I'm here on a mission, I want to heal my wrongdoings, that is if I'm not too late," said Charles. "Nothing is ever too late. If it has been recognised, you still have time to make amends." "Thank you, young man," replied Lord Charles. This gave him a much-needed boost. Was this true, could he heal the rifts he had caused? He watched the young man leave; his sister Rose had certainly picked herself a nice husband. Why had he said all those terrible things to this young man? Where to from here? he asked himself.

The next morning, Lord Charles hired a carriage and driver for the day to take him around the area so he could see more wheat paddocks. He couldn't believe how polite the people were; the lady from the inn had made him a packed lunch to take. "You must have food in your belly, young man," she told him. The driver asked him where he wanted to go. "Do you know a Mary O'Leary?" Charles asked. "Yes, everyone knows Mary, she is our saviour. She has battled for the tenant farmers, they feel indebted to her. Her family are well respected around here. Her husband, Connor, and the young man that works with him at the workshop are kept busy. The young man is a qualified engineer, so they get all the official jobs. Do you know them?" he asked. "I only know of them. Can we drive past their home?" asked Charles. "Right you are, sir." With this they were on their way. He was amazed at the acres of wheat, the crops looked so healthy, this being due to the Irish soil being so fertile, and the suitable weather. As they drove out to the Drinagh area, the driver pulled up at a gateway. It was a picture with its homemade gates and iron sculptures. "This belongs to Brendon and Rose Carey. Rose is Mary's daughter. Brendon makes things from scrap metal, people come from miles to buy his creations," the driver told Charles. "Do they have any children?" asked Charles. "Yes, they have two children who attend the local Catholic school."

They proceeded further on to the Curraghnaloughra area. It was also a wheat-growing area, and the crops could be seen for miles. "This is the start of the O'Leary farms; the twin sons work two farms together. Mary begins a little further on, but see that big building on the horizon? That is the workshop that belongs to Connor. It is one of the best businesses in the area, mainly because the grandson is a very talented young man. One of the best actually!" said the driver. "Oh, you know him?" asked Charles. "Just last week I had to take a shaft in to be fixed. He is a very obliging young man. Actually, he is due to marry a local Irish lass soon. There has been no talk of his family coming across the Irish Sea, which would be a pity, as he is a lad to be proud of." Lord Charles put his hand to his eye to wipe away a stray tear that had escaped.

As they drew closer to the workshop, a cart was coming down the driveway towards them. "There's young John, he is probably delivering a finished job," called the driver. Lord Charles strained to see if he could catch a glimpse of his son. There driving the horses was a strapping young man with a beard, an Irish one at that; he was quite a handsome lad. He saw Elizabeth in his features. This was the little child he had sent to boarding at the age of five and had very little contact with since. Suddenly a pain shot through his chest and he slumped forward. He couldn't get air, so he called to the driver, "Help me, help me!" but his pleas for help went unheard. "There's Mary's home, her gardens are open to all who want to visit, roses are her favourite flowers ..." and he kept up his commentary, but there was no response, so he pulled the horses to a stop and looked in the carriage, only to find his passenger slumped on the seat. He needed help, what would he do? The nearest home was Mary's so he whipped the horses and they trotted up the driveway.

When he reached the home, he called for help. Mary came rushing out. "What is wrong?" she asked. The driver explained he had a passenger who had taken ill, he needed help. Mary rushed to the carriage and when she opened the door there was a man slumped across the seat. She couldn't see his face, but she knew he was sick. "Help me get him inside," she told the driver. Between the two of them they managed to drag him inside and lay him on a bed. Mary ran to get a flannel to bathe his forehead. When she returned and bent down to attend to him, she couldn't believe what she saw. She was in shock. Lying on the bed was Charles, her son, whom she hadn't seen for many years. He looked old before his time, thus causing tears to flow down her cheeks. She asked the driver to go back to town and tell a doctor he was needed, as she didn't think it was the right thing to move him.

Mary knelt down and sponged his brow. She couldn't stop her tears from flowing; that maternal feeling had come back, it had never completely left. As much as she thought she disliked him, he was still her son, hers and Albert's. Why was he here, where was he staying, was he going to be all right? She took him in her arms and cradled him like she would a baby, and her tears fell on his face. He looked much older than his forty-eight years. What had happened to him? She was still holding him when the doctor arrived. "Who do we have here, Mary?" "Please, doctor, tell me what is wrong with him," she asked through her tears. The doctor did an examination but could not find anything majorly wrong with him. "I think he has collapsed with exhaustion, he needs to rest. Look at his eyes, they are so red, he looks as if he has a heavy heart," said the doctor. "Is he all right here with you, Mary?" "Yes, I will look after him," she answered. As the doctor took his leave, he told Mary to make sure he came in for a check-up after a couple of days' rest. She went back and sat on the bed beside Charles and took his hand. What has happened to you, my dear boy? she asked herself as she looked at his sallow face. He must have come to make his peace with John and Lucy, but how would they feel? He had not been part of their lives for many years, in fact he was only a memory. Could time heal? What was the future going to bring to this broken family? Would they be as forgiving as Mary?

Mary would not leave Charles's side. She sat with him hoping he would wake up. She bent down to kiss his forehead and at that very moment he stirred. As he opened his eyes, there was his mother bending over him. He closed his eyes again, as he thought he was dreaming. He had no idea where he was or what had happened. Then he heard his mother's voice: "My dear Charles, you are safe, don't be afraid." He was still dreaming, how he wished his mother was with him, she sounded so real. Mary tucked him in and left the room. The tears wouldn't stop. He had everything he wanted, the title, the Rothchild estate, children, but his face didn't portray that of a happy man. It was more like a man who had lost everything including his self-worth. She stood outside his door; she wanted to go back in, but her tears kept coming.

How was Mary going to explain to Lucy that her father was in their home? How would she feel? Her head was in a spin. But the person it would most affect would be Connor. He had been robbed of his son all those years ago and had never come to terms with losing him. Having John helped ease the pain, he was the son Connor dreamt of, but the grief had never left him. How was he going to feel when he knew Charles was here? Mary had never thought of this scenario. She had not overlooked the fact that Charles had hurt her family so many times, but he was still her son. Then there was John, the innocent one in all of this, and the one most loved by everyone. He had never been part of his father's life, he was the 'Irish curse' that had to be gotten rid of, out of sight out of mind. How would he feel? She still had several hours before any of the family came home. Connor and John had taken a packed lunch to work today, as they had deliveries to do.

Mary went back to the room where Charles lay. When she opened the door, he was sitting on the bed staring at the ceiling, still looking dazed. When he saw his mother, he tried to hide his face, then realised his dream had turned to reality. What was he doing here? All his demons filled his head, the tears flowed, the guilt and shame were all engulfing him, he felt so ashamed. "Mother, forgive me,

I'm so sorry," he sobbed. Mary looked at him: his face was drawn, he looked a broken man, tears stained his face and he hung his head in shame. "Charles, tell me what has happened." She sat down beside him and put her arms around him. "I have no-one, mother, I am alone, please help me. Will John and Lucy ever forgive me?" he asked. Mary could not answer for his children, but she could accept his forgiveness, after all he was her and Albert's son, their only child. "I can't stay here, mother, I am staying at the inn in town. Please take me there, I need time to recover. I couldn't face Connor, he must hate me. I have hurt everyone deeply, but I have changed. I hope it's not too late to make amends. 'Too late' — what did he mean by this? Was he sick? "I can't let you go, Charles, you don't look well."

"Please, mother, I must leave. I need time to think, take me to the inn," he asked of her. Mary could see he was not well enough to meet anyone, he needed rest. She told him she would bring the carriage to the front entrance and take him into town. He straightened himself up and walked to the front door, where Mary helped him onto the carriage. He wanted to sit up front so he could talk to his mother. As they were nearing the end of the driveway, a horse and cart was turning in and coming towards them. "Charles, this is John returning." "I will pull down my hat and hide my head, I can't let him see me like this," he pleaded. As they passed, Mary called out to him, "Where have you been, John, another finished job?" she asked. "Yes, grandmother, another happy customer. Where are you going?" he asked. "I'm taking a friend back to town, I will see you later!" she yelled as they drove on. "Charles, you and Elizabeth produced a lovely son. John has brought such happiness to our home. He took over Joseph's place in Connor's heart. You took from us, but you gave back to us. Please find it in your heart to make amends with him and Lucy. They have stayed close to each other, both having lost their respective mothers. Need I say more? I can't add more hurt, you have suffered enough.

How is the Rothchild estate?" she asked. "It's fine, mother, it misses your tender touch. It has never been quite the same since you left. But you have a lovely property here. Are you happy living in Ireland?" "Yes, Charles, this is my homeland, these are my people. All my life I made a promise to myself, that I would look after my people. They have suffered so much over the years, that is why I had to come home, my purpose in life has been fulfilled," Mary said with a happy heart. "You are so blessed, mother, I feel so ashamed not just with my personal life but with life in general. To see the state of the dwellings the tenant farmers live in is disgraceful. I should have listened to you, but I was selfish and arrogant. It has left me a lonely man without loved ones and despised by many, but this will all change. I am taking stock of my life and turning it around. I will need your help with John and Lucy and Connor." "Yes, my son, I will help you as much as I can, but first you must rest and get well," she told him.

As they rode into town, people were calling out to Mary, thanking her and wishing her a pleasant day. Charles could see his mother was loved by the townspeople. "You know, I can't get over how polite the Irish people are. Why did I think I hated them? That has been with me most of my life, how utterly wrong I have been. Tell me, mother, I went to the churchyard to put flowers on Joseph's grave. Why was he buried as Joseph O'Leary?" Mary told Charles the whole story, that he was the only child that she and Albert had together. Then she remembered Brendon telling them yesterday about the old man sitting on the seat crying at the churchyard. This must have been Charles. No wonder Brendon didn't recognise him, he looked so old.

As they pulled up outside the inn, Mary tethered the horses and went in with Charles. She knew the innkeeper, as she had stayed there many times. "How was your day, sir?" she asked Charles. Mary explained that he had taken ill and needed to rest for a couple of days. "I will check on him, Mary," she told her. They didn't tell her the connection, it was too soon. Mary hugged Charles and kissed him on the cheek. "I'm proud of you, Charles, you have seen your shortcomings, now you are making amends. Your life will turn around and you will find joy someday, but you must be patient." "Thank you, mother, you are still the maternal loving person I once knew, but chose to ignore. You are my saviour. Come and visit me in a couple of days. I must rest and get better." He held on to Mary as if it was his last goodbye!

Mary made her way home. Her heart was singing, she had made peace with her estranged son. At last he had realised the heartache he had brought to his family, but would they forgive him, as she had? How was she going to hide this from them? No-one had spoken of Charles for years, as they didn't want to bring his name up in front of his children, so Mary had no idea how they felt. Perhaps it was time to let his name resurface, to see how John and Lucy reacted. But her biggest worry was Connor. Would he still be bitter now that he had an extended family and grandchildren that he loved? Perhaps he had mellowed. Connor and Mary were in their mid-seventies. She hoped with age, he could find forgiveness in his heart. Charles was her only link to Albert, he was the one that provided her with the wealth they were all sharing today. She hoped this would be remembered by all. If that English lord had not helped that poor Irish girl all those years ago, where would they have been today?

That night at supper Mary brought up the subject that Brendon had mentioned to her a couple of days ago. "I keep wondering who that man was that was sitting on the seat in the churchyard, in front of Joseph's grave crying. He must have been lonely. I have been trying to think who it might be. Who would have known him back then? Brendon asked him what he was doing and he told him he was here to fix his wrongdoings." "I wonder if it was father. Perhaps now that he is older, he misses John and me. Wouldn't that be nice, John?" Lucy asked him. "I often wonder what has happened to him. George said in his last letter that he saw him and he looked old, he was drinking heavily. His last wife left him, perhaps he is lonely. But I don't think he would come to Ireland, he hates the Irish." Mary was waiting to see what Connor's reaction was. Then his feelings were revealed. "I can't see Charles ever coming to Ireland given his hatred for our people. But if he has, then one must think he is serving his penance, seeking forgiveness from those he has hurt. I know what it is like to hang on to hurt and hope for revenge; it destroys one's soul. Revenge is in retaliation of wrong done, but one must let it go, it does not help one to heal." Now that Mary knew everyone's feelings, she continued: "If it was Charles, could we all find it in our hearts to forgive him? It will be hard for you, John and Lucy, as you were both abandoned by him, but take time and think about it. Forgiveness is a pardon, it is a wonderful healing tool for us all."

Two days later Mary took the carriage into town; her

first call was to see Charles. She knocked on his door. "Come in," he called. Today he looked much better, a little colour was coming back into his cheeks, taking away the paleness that made him look ill. He had rested for the past few days and he had not consumed any alcohol; he couldn't believe how it had clouded his mind. All it did was cover up problems for a short period of time, but once it wore off the problems came back. It was only a short-term fix, this he understood now. "Mother, I have decided to go to the Titles Office and find out where my farms are. I was deeply affected by what I saw, the poverty of the tenant farms won't leave my mind. They are living in dwellings that are falling down. How can the men work all day while their families live in such hovels? I am going to make their homes comfortable and warm. All those years I have been so arrogant, I wish I had your kindness, mother," he told her. "Your children have inherited the Irish genes, Charles, that come with the 'Irish blessing'," Mary let him know. "My daughter Alice has the Irish hair." "Where is she?" Mary asked. Charles told his mother the story, not why Catherine left, but that she had found a better man than him. Now Mary could understand why he was at a low ebb. He had been abandoned, and now he knew what it felt like. Was it guilt that brought him to Ireland? "I have some news for you. I tested the family and they all seem ready to accept your forgiveness if you ever came to Ireland, even Connor, so it won't be long and I will arrange a family supper. "Thank you, mother. How sad that all these years have passed and we have been virtual strangers, but that is all behind us now," Charles said as he hugged his mother. He felt safe in her arms; there were no expectations!

For the next few days Charles was kept busy. He visited

the Titles Office and found out where his farms were situated. He had eight in total. He hired a carriage and driver to take him past each of his farms and was shocked by what he saw. The dwellings were no more than mud-brick hovels. Some housed up to six people, but where did they all sleep? "Not a good look, sir, those poor families. They work hard for the English gentry, then to have to come home at night to such poverty. It's a pity they didn't come over and see the conditions these humble people are living in. Surely, they have some responsibility to their workers, but this has been ongoing for many years, nothing seems to change," he said. Lord Charles was sitting up front with the driver, as it was a warm day. He couldn't hide his tears; he was one of whom had just been described. "Are you all right, sir?" enquired the driver. "Yes, thank you, I have never seen such poverty, but this will change, it can't stay like this. It must be made known to the landowners, what life is like here for their tenant farmers. It's all wrong, but one has to see to believe!" He thought of his own life of luxury, then what his mother had fought for to give her people a decent chance at life. How the Irish must despise the English aristocracy. And rightly so!

He asked the driver if he knew if any of the O'Leary farms were close by. "Now there's a fine woman. She came back from England after marrying a lord. She remembered her people and brought her wealth back and shared it with them. This is one of her farms on our right now. Look at the dwelling, she has such pride in her farms. Her farmers are the lucky ones, they all hold her in high esteem." Charles was amazed at the difference; there were even beds of roses, Mary's trademark. "Look at the gardens," remarked Lord Charles. "Yes, Mary gifted them the roses, hoping to bring a little joy to the hearts of the farmers' wives. She has a kind heart, she is of true Irish stock. She has even brought up several of her grandchildren, I don't know why, perhaps their parents have died?" the driver remarked. "Stop, driver! I will sit inside the carriage," instructed Lord Charles. The last statement made by the driver hit him right where it hurt most, in his heart. Did people think John and Lucy were orphans, being brought up by their grandmother? He wanted to own up to the driver and tell him he was one of those selfish gentry and those were his children, but instead, he took out his handkerchief and filled it with tears. He was again swamped by shame.

Tonight, after supper Mary was going to drop a bombshell. The time had come. She couldn't hide her secret any longer, it had to be shared. After they had all eaten, she asked them to meet in the drawing room, as she wanted to share something with them. John and Lucy were excited; what did Grandmother want to share with them? They had noticed she had been really happy the last few weeks. "I don't know how to begin, or what you are going to feel when I tell you my news, but please sit and think before you say anything. John and Lucy, your father is here in Ireland, in fact he is here in Dunmanway. He has been here for a couple of weeks recovering, as he was not well when he arrived." "Father here in Dunmanway? Can we see him?" yelled an excited Lucy. Mary was stunned by Lucy's acceptance, after all that he had put her through, but this was her forgiving nature. John and Connor looked at each other, neither able to say anything. "How do you feel, John?" asked Mary.

"Why has he come here?" he asked. Mary told them that he was doing his penance. His life had let him down badly, he was lonely and wanted to ask for forgiveness from those he had hurt. He had changed, he realised that all those close to him he has driven away through his own arrogance, now he has no-one. He is a lonely man and looks old and sad. He has been working out at his farm dwellings with the builders. He was shocked by the poverty that his tenant farmers had endured, so he is helping put things right. "Do you think, Connor and John, you could find it in your hearts to welcome him into our home for supper one night? We will have a family supper and if it all works out, we will have a celebration with his siblings and their families. But for the time being, this stays within these walls," said Mary. "Please, John and grandfather, let father have supper with us?" cried Lucy. "He must need us." This was all it took for them to agree, that Charles would be welcome as a guest in their home.

Tonight, was the night. It was Saturday so Lucy was not at college. She was so excited, she was looking forward to seeing her father. What would he think of her? She was sixteen now, she was only eight when her mother wrote to her grandmother Mary, asking if she could come to Ireland to live. She tried to remember her father. She had forgotten; fancy not remembering what her own father looked like. This made her sad. But Lucy didn't need to feel sad or guilty, she was the innocent one! It was her father who was the guilty one. John and Connor were in their workshop, neither had much to say to each other, as they were both deep in thought as to what was going to eventuate tonight. Deep down John felt he could forgive his father, simply because of his grandmother, as he was her son. His grandfather Rothchild had left his grandmother Mary well off and they had all benefited from this. He didn't hold any malice towards his father, because he was like a stranger. He never really got to know him, so felt he couldn't judge someone he didn't really know. The Irish blood ran full-bodied through John's veins, his life was one of acceptance, it had to be. His favourite people were his mother Elizabeth, George, Anne, his half-siblings and most of all his grandparents. His father was not on his list, simply because he hadn't earned that privilege!

Lucy was dressed in her Sunday best and looked lovely. No-one noticed her scarred face, it was just part of Lucy. John had trimmed his beard, as he wanted to look tidy to meet his father. And Connor, he hoped he could change his mind on Charles, or would the hurt come flooding back? There was so much at stake here. They were all waiting in the drawing room for Charles to arrive. Mary was on edge, wondering which way it would go. Was it tipping towards disaster, or success? She heard the doorbell chime so went to meet Charles. He took her in his arms. "Please help me, mother," he whispered. The tears weren't far off, she could see them forming in his eyes. He was frightened, these were family members he had deeply hurt. Would they forgive him?

"Come, Charles, your family are waiting." They walked hand in hand into the drawing room. Lucy couldn't believe her eyes; was this her father? He looked old and sad. "Father, is that you?" she cried as she ran to him. This was the first time he had had physical contact with his daughter; she felt warm and welcoming. He clung to her and they both cried together. John looked on. Who was this sad-looking man? He was a total stranger. His heart was torn to shreds; all he could see was suffering in his eyes, his face was pinched and his body was stooped. But he wasn't even fifty years old yet, what had happened to him? John remembered him as a self-righteous man, who held himself in high esteem. But before him stood a broken man, whose self-worth had plummeted. Suddenly their eyes met, and John couldn't turn away. His father's eyes were red and swollen, there was a plea there for forgiveness. John was now a man himself, so this became a man-to-man moment. Secretly, this was his one wish, to confront his father, but in this moment, everything was forgotten; forgiveness had taken over and this man-to-man moment brought them together. John went to him and held him; he felt frail, not like a father, more like a homeless being who had lost everything, even his soul. Mary's heart was racing; all these years she had dreamt of this coming together of her family, but she wasn't prepared for such emotion. The three estranged family members were huddled together, Lucy's cry was heard above all. All these years she felt her father had blamed her for Albert's death, that it was her fault, and now she had his forgiveness. She felt free of this burden. But to Charles this was not about Albert, it was about the way he had treated his daughter and now she had forgiven him, he was the one who had been freed!

The only person left was Connor. Charles approached him and held out his hand, waiting for him to shake it, as an acceptance of forgiveness. Mary watched on with bated breath. Had her husband let go of his hate for this man? There was nothing she could do, other than pray that he had it in his heart to accept Charles's hand. Silence befell the room. Charles's hand was still extended, then Connor made his move. He ignored the hand and took Charles in his arms and hugged him. This was more than Mary could have hoped for. Lucy ran to Mary and she held her in her arms. "Thank you, Grandmother Mary, for bringing our father here, you are the best friend John and I have."

This brought smiles to everyone, even Charles, who could have been hurt by this comment, but he was grateful his children had a loving and stable environment, something he couldn't provide for them. He was the failure in all this, and although he had it all given to him on a silver platter, he had abused his privileges and the people who had been part of his life.

17

Privilege Replaced by Compassion

~

Charles stayed on in Ireland with his family for three months. Bonds were forming and he felt happy for the first time ever. He had found his peace. He had met his siblings and their families and all had been forgiven. His health had improved, as he hadn't so much as touched alcohol since he crossed the Irish Sea. He had no need for it any more. John requested that Charles be there with him on his wedding day. Lucy was a bridesmaid and of course she wanted her father to be there for this special occasion. Charles knew that George had been invited; how would he feel when he saw him again? The ceremony was held in Mary's garden, it was an open affair and most of the village came to celebrate. The bride was a lovely Irish lass who John had met while at college. It was a lovely day and Charles was really happy to be part of this celebration.

Then he saw George. He was on his own, of course he wouldn't bring his partner along, as this was a dark secret that none of the family, apart from Rose, knew about. George was speaking to John, then they hugged each other. This hurt Charles; John was his son! George looked at Charles then made his way over to speak to him. "Congratulations, Lord Charles, I see you have done your penance.What a different man you look. Have you realised that by giving out kindness, it comes back in so many different ways? Titles and wealth are but words with no meanings; feelings come from within, they make your heart warm with happiness." It was only then that Charles realised for all the time he had spent in Ireland, his title of Lord had not been mentioned, until now, by George. All his young life he fought for this title, just to be someone, but now he was happier without it. Lucy came up to her father and asked him to come and have his photo taken with her and John. "Goodbye, Lord Charles. Now that you have your family, respect them and they will respect you back. Don't lose them again," said George, hoping he had learnt a lesson from his past.

His health was on the mend, it was the alcohol that was dragging him down. Now that was not a problem, his life had changed, he was now a happy man. Each day he would go out to his farms and help the builders to turn the broken-down dwellings into livable warm homes. The happy vibes from the tenant farmers and their families passed on to Charles, and it was then he realised his happiness was coming from helping people of a lesser standing than him. Even the Rothchild estate never aroused these feelings within him. He had it all moneywise, but his self-worth and happiness had left him. Charles had some serious thinking to do when he went back across the Irish Sea to England. He knew now, after spending time with his family, none of them would even think of coming back to the Rothchild estate; they had made their lives in Ireland.

The family had come to see Charles off, as he was returning to England. Lucy didn't want her father to leave, she begged him to stay, but he had business to attend to. John and Charles had forged a bond and spent quality time sitting on the river bank, trying their hand at fishing; sometimes they were lucky, other times not. But it wasn't the catch that was important, it was the father-son bonding. It had taken Charles time to realise that the most pleasures in life came without a price; they came from within and were free, it was just a matter of seeking and giving. There were hugs and handshakes all round, then the ferry blew its whistle signalling for the passengers to board, as shortly it would be on its way across the Irish Sea to England.

Back at the Rothchild estate, Lord Charles sat in his office and looked out the window. He had been home a month and his renewed zest for life was slowly seeping from his body. Several times he had lifted down the whisky bottle; he was tempted, but had the willpower to put it back. But how long could he hold off that temptation? He was missing his family, that was where he had found his happiness and his peace. He had called a meeting of the gentry to be held in his boardroom on Thursday. In his heart he knew he had to do battle for the tenant farmers, hoping to persuade the gentry to come on board with him. It was going to be a hard call, as it was only because he had seen the poverty for himself, but most of the landowners had never been to Ireland so hadn't see that side of life. Would his words be enough to sway them to his way of thinking?

He thought back to his earlier days, when nothing would have changed his thoughts on the tenant farmers. 'Make them pay, we as gentry need the money more than them', but how wrong was this? It was all back to front now that he had seen first-hand the suffering they had endured. It was going to be hard work to persuade his fellow landowners to come around to his way of thinking, but he would try his hardest to make them see things in a new light. Surely, they would listen to him?

Today was the board meeting and all the gentry arrived in their carriages. The gardener was there to tether the horses. Lord Charles greeted them and asked them to be seated. Even his neighbouring estate owner, Dr Michael, had come, but this was not a problem for Lord Charles. His life had moved on, he had accepted what had happened. After the business was seen to, it was now discussion time. Lord Charles started by telling the gentry what he had seen in Ireland, the hovels that their tenant farmers were expected to live in. He was so ashamed to be associated with such poverty, he had hired builders to make his farm dwellings into comfortable warm homes for his people. The mood of the meeting was sombre. "If we have to fix their homes, then we will have to look at increasing their land tariffs to recover our investment," someone suggested. "But we are not fixing their homes, they are our homes, we are responsible for our own properties. Besides, they are barely making a living now, we can't take any more from them. This would be a gesture of good faith without any rewards to us, but a better standard of living for them," replied Lord Charles. "Yes, I for one agree, we have neglected them for many years, now it is time to give back. I have seen the poverty these people are suffering; we have taken, but never given. Think about this seriously, then we should take a vote," said Dr Michael. The room was abuzz with discussion as the men mulled over their own positions. Would it mean they would have to budget their expenditure? Would it mean less for them? "Right, fellow gentlemen, we will have a show of hands," Lord Charles announced. He was disappointed with the outcome, as the majority voted against spending money without an increase in the tariffs to the farmers.

This was the turning point for Lord Charles. He had not been happy since his return from Ireland. He missed John and Lucy, they were his future, as were the Irish people. He could help so many poor people with his wealth. None of his family would ever come back to England, the Rothchild estate was no more than a name, not a happy one at that, so there was only one thing left ... sell and take his wealth across the sea to Ireland, as his mother Mary had done. The Rothchild estate would cease, a family tradition would be lost forever, he would give up his peerage, all so he could be reunited with his family. He knew he was not a well man, so the time he had left, he wanted to spend with them. He knew he had left it too late really, but he would try to salvage what precious time he could and enjoy all that he had missed out on over many years. He was happy he had made up with his mother, Mary, as she was his salvation when it came to caring for his children. She loved them and they loved her in return. He would never take another wife or partner, he had been hurt so many times by both sexes. But this was all of his own doing!

Of course, when word of Lord Charles's decision to sell and move to Ireland circulated among the gentry, they were in disbelief. Where were the future board meetings going to be held? But more importantly, what was going to happen to his farms? Would he sell them to the gentry? No, he was going to keep the farms and farm them from Ireland, which meant his yield would not come back across the Irish Sea. What of the gentry's bargaining power? It would diminish once again. They were up in arms; how could he do this to them? The sale would include the mansion and its surrounding land. This would be a desirable property for a wealthy gentleman. Only after making this announcement did Lord Charles see that no-one really cared about him; if there wasn't gain in it for them, then he was on his own. He sold his law practice to his staff, as they had helped build it into the thriving business it was today. His move was getting closer!

Lord Charles's estate was viewed by many wealthy gentlemen. It was a top property, the gardens were beautiful, the sunken rose beds had been there for several generations, and cared for in a most loving manner. The stables and the outbuildings were in top order, no expense had been spared on the property. It was bringing much interest, not just locally but from the far north of the country. This was a once-in-a-lifetime sale, as most estates passed down from one generation to the next, so to find this prime real estate was indeed a must have. There were new offers coming in all the time but tomorrow was the cut-off date. The property would go to the highest bidder. When the agent came to Lord Charles with the highest offer, he was astounded; he did not think for one moment it was worth the amount of money he was offered. Of course, he didn't hesitate; the price was accepted.

He was leaving all the chattels in the house but for one item, the piano he had bought as a wedding present for Elizabeth, John's mother. He thought this would be a reminder for John of his mother, not remembering that John was sent to boarding school at aged five, just after his mother had died, so his memories were very vague of his mother, let alone the piano! Lord Charles thought it might be used again one day, when John and his bride had children. Then he remembered that Sarah and Lucy learnt to play, but his arrogant manner at the time forbade them to play it, as it belonged to his first wife. Perhaps if Lucy wanted to play again, she could use it until John needed it. He kept telling himself he had to leave his past behind. It had been unpleasant, he had been unpleasant, he didn't want to return there! He was a different person now, he viewed life in a happier perspective, realising there was more to life than just himself. Other people made him happy, he couldn't do it on his own, and wealth certainly didn't help him either. His life was proof of that!

Lord Charles was not going to miss the estate; it brought loneliness and many unpleasant memories. The good times with George were marred by what he thought of Lord Charles, revealed in his letter. All he felt about their relationship was shame, as his behaviour had turned George against him. He couldn't even hold the love of his life; what sort of man was he?

All memories that made Charles sad, he planned to leave behind in England. He was now plain Charles Rothchild; the peerage was gone, it wasn't relevant any more, it was not going to be part of his new life. He was on the ferry crossing the Irish Sea and was looking forward to a new life in his adopted Ireland. It was a new beginning! He was looking forward to spending time with John and

Lucy. John had moved out from his grandparents' home and had settled on a new property with his Irish bride. Mary asked her son to come and live with her and Connor on their property, but Charles couldn't let go of the gross injustice he had caused Joseph; he thought he could see it was still there in Connor's eyes. As the ferry docked at the wharf, Charles hailed a carriage to take him to Dunmanway. He hadn't let the family know what day he was arriving, as he wanted to take his own time to sort things out. The carriage driver took him to the inn he had stayed at when he was last in Dunmanway. The innkeeper remembered him. "You look much better this time, sir," she greeted him.

The next morning, he walked up to the churchyard with a bunch of flowers to leave at Joseph's headstone. He sat on the seat and cried for this innocent life he had taken to feather his own nest. While he was sitting there another visitor arrived; it was his half-sister Rose. She knelt by Joseph's grave and prayed for him. She hadn't seen Charles there until she stood up. They looked at each other, then Charles asked her to come and sit with him. Silence reigned for a few minutes, then Rose came and sat down. "I'm sorry, Rose, for the heartache I have caused this family. I can't change things, it is too late, but I have suffered. I come here to Joseph's grave and hate myself for what happened," he sobbed. "We have forgiven you, Charles. Time heals wounds, as deep as they may have been," she told him.

Now was her chance to talk to Charles privately. "I know about your secret life, I've known since your twenty-first. One of your friends left a letter addressed to me under a pillow, explaining what you were. I have kept this to myself all these years, not even Brendon knows. I know

about George; what happened that you are not together?"
Rose asked. She knew why they had broken up, as she
had met and spoken to George when he brought John to
see his grandmother; she wanted to see Charles's reaction.
Just the mention of his secret affair and George churned
inside Charles; he couldn't hide his tears. "He was the love
of my life, but like everyone else I chased him away. He
left me to look after John. In the end, he hated me for
the way I treated my son. I have made a mess of my life,
hence my suffering, but I can blame no-one else other than
myself. I am so grateful my children have accepted me,
and that my family have forgiven me. I am a very wealthy
man but I am going to help the impoverished people of
Ireland. The Rothchild estate is no more, it has gone, as
has my lordship. I am now a humble man who wants to put
right my wrongdoings from the past." "But, Charles, you
hated the Irish, all your life you voiced how you felt about
them. You raised the farmers' land tariffs and made them
suffer, so you could live the life of a gentleman. What
changed you?" asked Rose. "The day I stepped foot on
Irish soil, everyone was so kind to me. They didn't even
know me, but that didn't matter. A warmth was generated
in my heart, something I had never felt before. Then I
took a carriage and saw the broken-down dwellings that
these people lived in, it broke my heart. I worried for the
children. Were they being fed? Were they cold? It brought
me back to reality. I didn't even care for my children; all
the wealth in the world and I cast them aside and told
them they had the 'Irish curse'. How cruel was that? They
were innocent children, and all the time it was because
of me they had Irish blood. I will always remember what
Catherine, my third wife, told me: 'I can only give you
what you give me'. I blamed everyone else, not admitting

that all the time the blame lay with me. I live with this every day and suffer I must do, it is my penance!"

Rose listened with interest. Here was her half-brother admitting to his wrongdoings. She remembered him as an arrogant child who grew into an arrogant aristocrat and fought all out to get his peerage. It was his by right and at any cost, the cost being Joseph, who lay before them buried in the churchyard. "I think, Charles, that Joseph has forgiven you. You have suffered like he had, but you were both young at the time. Now you are a grown man and faced up to your wrongdoings, put all this behind you and live the rest of your days with kindness in your heart. Mother is a fine example, we are blessed to be her children." "Thank you, Rose, this has brought great comfort to me, and yes, we have been blessed. Mother is very special to so many people; without her, where would my children have gone? I will follow her example and share my wealth with as many impoverished Irish people as I can." With this the two siblings stood and hugged each other. They both shared a secret that they would take to their graves, never to be revealed! At all cost, this secret was never to reach Mary's ears; she would never have forgiven herself to know she had borne a son of ill-repute.

Charles Rothchild, the privileged son born to Lord Albert and Mary Rothchild, had his life gifted to him on a silver platter. But sadly, his conceited attitude and his arrogance shown towards his family, especially to those of his own flesh and blood, and his imagined hatred towards the Irish, blurred his vision of who and what was important in his life. But when he was alone and all was lost to him, it was time for him to take a look at himself and see where it all went wrong. The blame lay solely within him, no-one else. Now all that was left was for him to rebuild and find it in his heart to ask forgiveness from the people he had hurt. To think he called his first-born son John, a name he gave him because of his Irish hair, a son who he didn't think was deserved of a Rothchild family name. A son he now loved dearly and who had grown into a respectable young man that everyone wanted a part of. How sad was that? he admitted to himself. All he could hope for now was his son might find it in his heart to use the Rothchild names Albert and Charles for any future sons that may be born into the family. Or was it too late? Were these names going to be lost forever to a new generation, leaving behind a turbulent past? And Lucy, what a loving girl. She was Irish through and through and Charles was proud that his Irish blood had passed on to her. He had found acceptance in his heart for his Irish heritage at long last!

But his one love, George, would never forgive Lord Charles for the cruelty he had imposed on his son John and his wife Elizabeth during his time on the estate. For Charles, life had to move forward. His wealth would be spent on improving living conditions for the tenant farmers; he would fight for them, to secure a better standard of living for them and their families. He had become a self-proclaimed Irishman; there was no hate left in his body, it had been replaced with kindness. He had his family now, this was all he needed, he had found his peace. His penance was served!

About the Author

Margaret Nyhon lives in Alexandra, in the Central Otago province of New Zealand, where she writes, paints and practises the crafts of printing and bookbinding. She has worked extensively in hospitality management in New Zealand and resort management in Australia. The urge to trace her family history led her to the writing of her first non-fiction work, *de Marisco*. She has since written several fiction and non-fiction works. Margaret is married and has three adult children and two grandsons.

Other Books by the Author

Non-fiction

de Marisco
Freedom Knows No Boundaries
A Wake-up Call
A Shattered Dream Across the Tasman

Fiction

Isobella (Book 1 in the *Isobella* series)
Isobella: Self Redemption (Book 2 in the *Isobella* series)
Papa's Girl Emmeline
Betrayal by an Irish Rose
For Girls' Eyes Only

Coming Soon

Pimchan's Journey Away From Poverty
Based on a true story
Daughters Lost to the Underworld